Pip of Pengersick –
a smuggler's tale

Titles available in the Pip series:

Pip of Pengersick – a smuggler's tale
La Bandida – Pip goes to Mexico *(not yet published)*

Tartu series:

Tartu and the Pharaoh's Curse
Tartu's Close Encounter
Tartu's Arctic Adventure *(not yet published)*

Zulu series:

Zulu Magregor and the vultures of San Felipe
(not yet published)

www.harveyberrickpublishing.co.uk

Pip of Pengersick – a smuggler's tale

J. A. C. WEST

HARVEY
BERRICK
PUBLISHING

First published in Great Britain in 2006
Reprinted October 2006
Reprinted January 2007

Harvey Berrick Publishing, 8 The Links, Pengersick Lane, Praa Sands, Cornwall TR20 9RD

Copyright © J.A.C. West 2006

The moral right of the author has been asserted
A CIP catalogue record of this book is available from the British Library

ISBN-10 0-9553150-2-6
ISBN-13 978-0-9553150-2-2

Printed in Great Britain by Headland Printers, Penzance
Designed by Nicky Stott and Alex Szyszkowski
Illustrations by Oliver Lake

To Mum and Dad, who always believed in me

Foreword

I was born in a castle – which makes me sound very grand. But it was a falling down sort of castle and my family were the only ones who lived there – with a few ghosts. We didn't bother them and they didn't bother us.

So it was just me, my mother and my ten brothers and sisters. Father was a salty seadog type who'd been on shore leave. Mother didn't talk about him much – but she said I looked like him, especially when I laughed. And I laughed quite often.

She named me 'Pip' after a character in a book. I never learned which.

I'm Pip of Pengersick and this is my tale.

CHAPTER 1

An honest trade

Smuggler: A person who though no doubt blameable for violating the laws of his country is frequently incapable of violating those of natural justice and would have been in every respect an excellent citizen had not the laws of his country made that a crime which Nature never meant to be.

Professor Adam Smith

When I was just a pup, Cornwall was a wild and lawless place. The roads were few and the people who travelled them were fewer still. Only the rich and the outlaws went on long journeys: the first paid with their own money; and the second paid with someone else's money – I couldn't really see much difference.

There was a third group of people who travelled a long way – the ones who got caught by the King's Customs Officers. They were sent to the Assizes in Launceston, which is another word for gaol, and found guilty (I don't remember anyone ever being found innocent), and they were sent off to Australia, which is a very long way from Cornwall. I only ever met one person who returned from Australia and it sounded like a terrible place on the other side of the world: fierce suns, nothing to eat, as barren as a rock, and with big animals that bounced along on their back legs. The one who told me swore he wasn't making it up, but I'm not so easily fooled.

Most of the folk earned their living from mining tin, fishing, farming or smuggling – some people did all four; but they were the God-fearing ones who liked to work hard. Fortunes were made and lost from the tin that they ripped from the stony ground or the pilchards that swam in shoals like quicksilver. But no-one made a fortune from farming – not unless they were the kind of farmers who made everyone else plough the fields and dig the vegetables and never got their own paws dirty.

Well, I wasn't much use down a tin mine and I didn't swim well enough to catch fish, so I decided from a very early age that my future lay in smuggling.

Of course, smuggling in those days was an honest trade and the people who smuggled goods were pretty much law-abiding souls – except that the law was a fool. Lawful rum, gin and brandy cost eight shillings a gallon, but you could buy it from the smugglers for three shillings and three pence. You tell me who were the thieves! The Customs men and the King said that smuggling was breaking the law, but Customs men wore fog glasses and were happy enough to take a bribe here and there; and as for the King, I reckoned he was rich enough – which I was surely not.

So at the tender of age of three months, I packed up my worldly belongings (an old bone and shred of blanket) and said goodbye to my mother, brothers and sisters. Mother washed my face carefully and my brothers and sisters crowded around giving me playful nips and said I should remember them if I ever got rich – which I fully intended to do. Then I turned my back on Pengersick Castle and left home to make my fortune.

⟫◦⟪

I followed the narrow lane that led uphill, away from the sea and the castle and was soon beyond my knowledge. I had heard the rattle of carts travelling up and down this road but had never before seen its wide, dusty expanse for myself. It stretched from East to West with no visible signs of habitation. For no particular reason I turned left and trotted along as the high road stretched out before me.

The road seemed very long and my young paws soon began to tire. I was hot and thirsty and missed my mum and the stream in the garden and the comfort of my brothers and sisters.

But I think I was born under a lucky star because I hadn't travelled much further down the big road, when I heard the sound of a horse's hooves behind me. A horse is a very big creature indeed to one as short as I, so I stepped off the road politely and waited for the horse and its rider to pass.

"Woah!" said the man, pulling the horse to a gentle stop. "Now what do we have here. That's a fine looking whelp to be sure," and he pointed at me. "Where are you going, young puppy dog?"

Of course, I was too young to have learned human speaking, so all his words sounded like a rumble of summer thunder to me. But his voice was kind and I looked up at him wagging my tail.

"Why don't you hitch a lift, young buckaroo?" said the man, and he got down off his great horse and scooped me up onto the saddle in front of him. The horse looked a bit annoyed at having an addition to his burden, but it seems to me that if you're as big as a horse then you shouldn't mind taking along a few hitch hikers; but now I think of it, you don't often see cows giving people a ride. They must be cleverer than horses, I think.

The sun was high in the sky when the man, the horse and I finally turned off the road. We hadn't seen a single other living soul as we rode along, even though I could hear rustlings in the high, old hedges that told me we were being watched.

The horse found his way without any guidance from the rider down a long, winding road that gradually became narrower and steeper. Well, it's a road nowadays, but then it was nothing more than a farm track: choked with dust in the summer and clogged with mud in the winter.

As the road sloped downwards, my nose began to twitch. I could smell salt in the air and the sound of the sea crashing onto the rocks reached my ears. The horse began to walk faster as if he knew his journey's end was near and a warm stable and comfortable straw awaited him.

As we rounded the corner, I caught my first sight of what was to be my new home. It wasn't as big as the castle where I had been born, but had the distinct advantages of a roof and doors. Smoke was rising steadily from the chimney and the whole place had a friendly, cosy air about it. A wooden sign above the door creaked gently in the morning breeze. It had a picture of a man with a long nose, sunken cheeks and haunted eyes. He was wearing a crown.

The man had dismounted the horse and tucked me inside his coat, when a boy came running out from the back of the house.

"Uncle Harry! You're home!"

"Awright, boy!" said Harry. "Take ole Jethro for me and fix him up proper, will you?"

The boy gave Harry a hug and trotted off with Jethro, who seemed extremely grateful to be rid of his riders.

Harry knocked on the door and pushed it open. I have one great advantage over people, despite my small size; I can see in the dark better than any cat. I saw at once that the man in the picture was sitting next to the fire. Except his eyes were just like

Harry's – kind and friendly – and he wasn't wearing a crown.

The two brothers embraced and nearly squashed me in the process. I let out a yelp.

"What have you got there, Harry?" said the other man.

"It's a little stray I found on the Penzance Road, John," he replied. "Thought we could train her up a bit and if she's a good ratter, she could make herself useful about the place."

"Bless you for a soft heart!" said John and laughed gently.

Harry laid me down on an old blanket in the corner and gave me a bowl of water and a slice of bacon, sizzling hot from the pan over the fire. I thought I must be in a palace, having never had such luxuries before. At home, water came from the stream at the bottom of the castle's tangled gardens or from the pools of rain that collected on the ground where the roof had fallen in. And I'd never had hot food before. What joy! I shall never forget that first sniff of a piece of frying delight. I wonder if the angels feed you bacon in Heaven?

I fell asleep, tired from the journey and the trials and tribulations of my first adventure. I was still just a young pup with nine long months of growing ahead of me.

I lay warm and comfortable on my new old blanket and listened to the sounds of habitation around me. Apart from Harry and John, there was John's son Tom (the boy who had seen to Jethro) and two daughters, Jenna and Jessie, plus his wife Margaret, known as Meg.

As the day passed, more men started arriving at the house. I could tell by their boots, striped jerseys, baggy trousers, overcoats and souwesters tucked into their pockets that they were seafaring men; and I could tell by the twitching in my tail that every man Jack of them was a smuggler!

"It'll be high tide in two hours and sundown in three," said

John… "and the moon just right tonight. 'Twill be dark enough."

"Right you are," said Harry. "Hear that, boys?"

Harry picked up his overcoat and a large leather bag that clinked softly.

I pricked up my ears at this – it sounded like an adventure. I gave a hopeful little bark and looked eagerly at Harry.

"Sounds like young 'un wants to go, too," said John.

Harry frowned. "I reckon she's a bit young – don't want any accidents."

"Oh go on," said John. "You said you wanted to train her up."

Harry smiled. "Right you are. Come on then, youngster," and he picked me up in one beefy hand and stuffed me inside his greatcoat. It was warm in there and I soon began to doze, rocked by the rhythm of his rolling gait. I was to learn that Harry rolled along like that whether he was on land or sea. I think he was happier at sea, on the whole.

The smugglers' boat was a lugger, which is a small vessel about 30 feet long with three masts and a large square sail. From a distance it looked like an ordinary fishing lug, but the masts were fixed and the hull was deeper than on a normal boat and the fishing nets disguised a small broadside cannon that could be brought to bear in times of trouble.

We were ready for anything. Well, Harry and his men were. I was still fast asleep.

The little boat sailed silently from Bessy's Cove. With the sail painted black we were all but invisible on the pitch-black sea. How Harry navigated that treacherous coast I'll never know; he was a man at the top of his profession.

We sailed all night. Just as dawn was breaking, Harry eased the boat into a small cove with a sandy beach and dropped the anchor. It was the tiny island of Bryher, some thirty miles from Land's End and one of a group that made up the Isles of Scilly; a most convenient stopping point for the smugglers' trade.

"Right, boys," said Harry. "We'll take turns to keep watch: Shem and Jacob you go first. The rest of you get some sleep."

I was rather disappointed at the lack of action; I thought the smugglers were going to charge up the beach shooting their guns and waving their cutlasses, fighting off all who opposed them. I came to learn that smugglers prefer to ply their trade as quietly as possible. Guns and shouts and cutlasses mean that the Customs men have got you in their sights. And that's no good thing.

But I was full awake after sleeping all night in Harry's coat. So I sat with Shem and Jacob who fed me bits of meat and potato that were wrapped up in a thick, golden pastry – these were Cornish pasties and I came to like them even better than bacon.

After a while two other men took over from Shem and Jacob and then two more. The day passed slowly and I dozed off and on in the warm summer sunshine, cooled by the breezes that blew steadily from the sea, and rocked by the gentle motion of the waves.

I couldn't tell you what first caught my attention, but suddenly I was completely alert. My nose twitched and my tail quivered. I let out a low growl deep in my throat, just like mother used to do when seagulls tried to steal her hard won food.

Instantly Harry was awake by my side. "What is it? What do you hear?"

My ears picked up the distant echo of hooves – lots of hooves – and they were coming from the low rise above us. I looked towards the sound and Harry understood me at once.

He muttered, "Well done, little maid," then in a louder voice, "We're on, lads. On your toes."

Although Harry and his men took the precaution of loading their pistols and loosening their cutlasses in the scabbards once they had clambered onto the beach, they were clearly expecting the newcomers.

Six mules tiptoed down the rocky path laden with heavy packs. They looked like horses but had longer ears and were considerably worse tempered. I didn't take to 'em and they surely didn't take to me. I kept my distance after one of the surly critters tried to kick me. We hadn't even been introduced.

"Evening, Harry," said the man leading the mules. Here's the moonshine if you've got the tin."

"You sure you got proper brandy there, Ned, and not any of that filthy stinkwater that you tried to sell me last time?"

"Would I do that to a friend?" said Ned, who looked shiftily from beneath astonishingly bushy eyebrows.

"Yas, I reckon you would," said Harry, and Ned looked annoyed.

Harry went up to the first pack and pried open the small barrel of brandy. He sniffed it and nodded. He then went on to test all the other barrels. Forty passed and seven were rejected with a shake of his head. By this time Ned was furious.

"There's nothing wrong with them there barrels!" he spat.

"Then you won't be having any trouble selling them, will you?" replied Harry calmly. "I pay top whack for my goods, but I won't be made a lubber-head neither." He held out the leather moneybag to Ned. "Take it or leave it; it's a fair price for 40 barrels."

Ned was spitting with fury, but snatched the moneybag and started back up the rise with his mules, "A curse on 'ee, Harry Carter," he snarled. "I'll not forget this."

"See that you don't," said Harry, "and don't try to cheat me again!"

The brandy was loaded into our lugger and hidden beneath some old lobster pots. I noticed that the boat now rode much lower in the water and looked far more like an ordinary fishing boat, its deeper hull hidden beneath the waves.

We were just about to weigh anchor when I sensed that we were not alone. I scanned the shoreline but could see nothing in the gathering gloom of evening. Perhaps old Ned had come back to hurt Harry. I wasn't going to let that happen. The hackles on the back of my neck rose and I growled fiercely, bearing my teeth. Not that my teeth could have hurt anyone much as they were still just baby teeth and some were falling out, but I did my best to look savage.

Harry looked at me in surprise. "Ole Ned's gone now, little maid," he said. But then he saw I was serious and looked about him for the source of my alarm. "Careful, lads," he hissed. "We're not alone."

Instantly, the men were on their guard.

A falling pebble drew Harry's attention upwards. He looked up at the rise above us, silhouetted in black against the sinking sun. A flash of sun on metal where metal ought not to be brought Harry to the full alert.

"Damn Ole Ned!" he shouted. "He's sold us out to the Customs men!"

Above us on the cliff, a row of soldiers in red coats appeared, their white cross-straps showing clearly in the gathering gloom, their muskets pointed right at us.

"Let's make a run for it, boys," yelled Harry. "They'll not get a good sight of us in this gloom. Weigh anchor!"

But at that moment a full-sized warship of the King's Navy sailed into view, blocking our escape. We were well and truly caught.

CHAPTER 2

The Tax Man cometh

But, whatever contrite admissions to this extent were extorted from old Tristram by misty glimpses of a moral sense, there were two points on which he was inexorably firm. The one was, that it was a very guilty practice in the authorities to demand taxes for what he called run goods; and the other was, that it never could be a sin to make away with an exciseman.

Reverend R S Hawker

We didn't stand a chance. With soldiers above us, and sailors beyond us, blocking our escape, there was nothing for it but to turn ourselves in.

"Ole Ned's curse has come true," said Jacob fearfully.

"Curse!" hissed Harry. "Curse! Indeed it is a curse for the old fool has turned us in to the Tax Man: Customs or Excise – I know not which, for one is as bad as t'other. Do you think it luck that made them pick this time and this place? No! I'd bet my boat that Ole Ned is behind this. But the silly old gammock is as fleeced as we. They'll be taking every farthing they can and turn him off without even a sniff of his own brandy stinkwater."

Harry was right. A yowling and howling reached my ears such as I have never heard from any human before or since. Ole Ned was being dragged down the slope by two burly soldiers who seemed not to care that his ancient bones were near pulled from his arm sockets. Harry frowned for he could not bear to see

unnecessary suffering to any creature, be it human or one such
as I.

"But I helped you!" whined Ole Ned to the soldiers who
marched him to captivity. "You promised that if I helped 'ee, I'd
go free! A sovereign, you promised!"

"You've been well and truly timdoodled, Ned," said Harry,
not unkindly. "I hope 'twas worth it."

"They made me!" wailed Ole Ned. "They made me do it!"

The captain of the Customs Men swaggered over. "I am
Captain Dollard," he said. "I've been waiting to catch you at
your tricks, and now I've got you; the reward of a patient man.
Better get ready to hang, Harry Carter," he said with a cold
smile.

"Well now," said Harry calmly. "I wouldn't say as I've been
'got' until I'm standing before the Justice at Launceston. There's
many a slip between cup and lip, or so I've been told."

"Yes, you're right," agreed the captain, slowly. "I don't doubt
you have equally guilty friends in both high and low places.
Well, perhaps I'll just hang you now and save the law the time
and trouble."

He pointed to his ship. "I think I'll hang you by the neck
from the yardarm so all can see you're just a lowlife smuggler; a
wretch; a thief; an unworthy citizen. Take this piece of filth
away."

Harry was white, though whether with anger or fear, I could
not tell. I bared my teeth at the captain and barked fiercely. He
lashed out viciously, kicking me hard in the ribs and I yelped
with pain.

Harry was beside himself and struggled against the two men
who held him. "She's just a pup!" he yelled. "Leave her alone!
Brute! Call yourself a man – you're very brave against a helpless

puppy! Come on and face me instead!"

But Captain Dollard just laughed in his face, "You've got till dawn to make your threats," he said, "then you die – and the whelp with you."

I was whimpering and trying to lick my ribs, but it hurt too much to move. When the captain wasn't looking, one of the soldiers scooped me up and wrapped me gently inside Harry's coat.

"I'll not forget this kindness, friend," whispered Harry.

A thin smile passed like a cloud over the soldier's face, then he shrugged his shoulders and walked away.

We were all loaded onto a small rowing boat and taken out to the waiting warship. From there, we were taken and thrown into the brig, which is what they call a prison on board a ship.

The brig was dark and damp and smelled of old seaweed. I could hear the scuttling of rat feet, but was too sore and dispirited to do more than growl softly.

Ole Ned was thrown in with us and lay cowering in the corner. Harry's men were all for doing him in there and then, but although Ole Ned was a traitor and a turncoat, Harry didn't have the heart to further reduce the old man and persuaded the others to let him be.

Then Harry picked me up and examined me carefully. I yelped when his finger touched my hurt rib. He gently stroked the damaged bone and I whined softly.

"Never mind, little maid," he said. "It's not broken, just badly bruised. You'll mend well enough." He raised his head and his expression hardened as he looked at his men. "I cannot abide a fellow who would hurt such a little creature."

The men agreed with him and discussed all the unpleasant things they would do to Captain Dollard, should they ever get the chance. But soon the talk turned to our present predicament.

"Try not to worry, lads," said Harry. "If this is it for me, then I shall make my peace with my maker. But remember, we have many friends on these islands and 'tis many hours till dawn."

His words gave comfort to the men – such was the trust they had in Harry. Like them, I was soon curled up and fast asleep.

Shortly after midnight, I was roused by a sound I knew well – the gentle splashing of oars and the creaking wood of a small boat. I was not the only one wide-awake. Harry was sitting bolt upright, listening intently. "They're coming," he said.

Silently, one by one, he woke the rest of the men. "Get ready, lads," he whispered. "I think we're about to be rescued."

I listened to the sound of bare feet slapping on the wooden deck above our heads. There was a muffled shout, a curse and the thud of an unconscious body falling to the deck.

"We're in here!" yelled Harry in a hoarse whisper. "Over here!"

Nervous fingers fumbled with the huge metal bolt on the roof of our prison and we were soon being pulled out on deck by eager hands.

"Quickly, Harry," cried one of the rescuers. "We've a couple of rowing boats secured at the stern."

But it was too late for a stealthy retreat. We'd been spotted.

"Smugglers!" yelled a voice. "We're being boarded!"

Shots rang out and flashes of orange illuminated the night. Soldiers poured from the hatches onto the quarterdeck, their heavy boots pounding the wooden boards, easily outnumbering us twenty to one, and armed to the teeth. We didn't have so much as a stick between us with which to beat them. There was no way we could fight.

"Over the side, lads!" yelled Harry.

At that moment I spotted Captain Dollard running onto the quarterdeck. My fury exploded and I leapt with all my might to sink my baby teeth into the well-padded white breeches of his backside.

He let out a satisfying yell, for my baby teeth, though small and some rather loose, were needle-sharp. I had my revenge and honours were even.

There was no time to climb down the ropes to the waiting boats. It was every man for himself. I ran, too, and plunged 30 feet through the night into the waiting darkness. The cold shocked me to the core and I swallowed a mouthful of salt water as I sank beneath the waves. I couldn't tell which way was up and I was more frightened than I had ever been in my entire life. I didn't want to die here in this cold and friendless place.

Kicking with my legs, I rose to the surface coughing and spluttering, only to sink beneath the darkness for a second time. I didn't have the strength to struggle any more and I sighed to think I would not see Harry or home again.

At that moment, I felt a hand reach down to grab me by the scruff of my neck, pulling me back to the surface, back to life.

"Hang on there, beauty," said Harry.

Shouts and yells sounded from the ship and some soldiers fired into the black water, the flashes from their muskets sending sparks into the night. Luckily most of the soldiers seemed to understand the pointless nature of firing at moving targets in a pitch-black sea.

I buried my nose in Harry's wet hair and clung on for dear life. He stuffed me inside his shirt and started swimming strongly. But the current was pulling us out to sea and I could tell that Harry was tiring.

"Hold on, boy!" cried a voice.

I heard the splashing of oars nearby and thought for the first time that we might survive this terrible night.

Strong arms plucked us from the sea and we collapsed into a heap in the bottom of a little rowing boat.

"Jory!" said Harry. "Thank goodness! I owe you my life!"

"Then we're even," said Jory heartily, "for you've done as much for me and my kith and kin."

"Are the rest of my boys ok?" asked Harry.

"We won't know that till we're back on land," said Jory. "I've

got four, with you, and two other boats joined me on the raid: Willy Nankerris and John Bosahon. I'll row us round to t'other side of Bryher. It's too shallow for their great ship to follow us. You'll be safe there."

"God bless you, Jory Tregarthens!" said Harry.

It was many hours before we were safely back on land.

Jory took us into his home, a tiny, stone-built cottage on the edge of the water. There was no harbour, just a strip of soft white sand. Harry and the men helped him pull his rowing boat up the beach and we thankfully entered his home and stood around the fire warming ourselves, for we were wet to the skin and almost perished with cold.

Jory's wife bustled around making tea and a hot, nourishing stew that consisted almost entirely of fish heads. Generous as they were with what little they had, I realised that these people were very poor indeed.

An old man, wizened and shrunk by the years, sat at the back of the darkened kitchen. It turned out that he was Jory's grandfather and the oldest of all Isles' folk.

"'Tis shameful," he said. "Shameful and wicked that you have been treated in this way, Harry Carter. If it were not for you and the business you bring to these islands, we would have starved long ago. The King cares nought for us, though these Isles belong to him. When the first King Charles was beheaded by the Republicans," he went on, spitting forcefully, "we protected his son, the new King. Us saved his life and what thanks do us get? Nothing! Nothing! We should have let him die and tried our luck with Cromwell's lot."

"Hush, grandfather!" said Jory's wife. "You're talking of things that happened a hundred year ago. 'Tis long gone. 'Tis now a different king, to be sure."

"They is all the same," wailed the old man. "What if it were a hundred year ago? My father was here. He helped save the King, but the King cares not for the likes of us. He sends his Customs Men," (here he spat again) "and tries to stop the only thing that keeps us fed and with clothes on our backs. He taxes our beer, cider and spirits. He taxes our salt, leather, and soap. He even taxes our tea so that we cannot afford it. He'd tax the very air we breathe, if he could."

Many of Harry's men nodded in agreement.

I had not thought deeply on the subject of smuggling until this moment. The furthest my thinking had taken me was that Harry was a good, kind man, whatever his job. But now I realised that these islanders were utterly dependent on the trade that Harry and those like him could bring them. This was why Jory had risked his life to free us from the hands of the Customs Men. Life was not so cheap that a man would just throw it away without good reason.

A knock at the kitchen door heralded the arrival of three more of Harry's men. By midday all Harry's crew had arrived at the little cottage and only Ole Ned was missing.

"He wouldn't dare show his face here," said Jory, "not if he knows what's good for him."

There was more good news; Harry's lugger was safe.

"We cut her lines and she beached herself just off Frenchman's Point on Tresco," said Jory. You'll be able to float her off at high tide."

Jory and his family were very kind to us and I particularly enjoyed sitting next to Jory's grandfather whilst he fed me tiny pieces of fish from the soup that bubbled continuously on the fire.

Jory's wife shook her head and tried to be cross but threw me a crust of bread when no-one was looking.

I was sorry indeed to say goodbye to them and I think the old man would have liked me to stay, but I had thrown in my lot with Harry and he had proved himself a true friend. It was not in my nature to forget a good turn, and Harry had saved my life. I was determined to pay him back.

It felt good to be back on board and sailing for home. Even the barrels of brandy had survived the marauding Customs Men. Just one barrel was missing and I wondered if its absence had accounted for the poor shooting of the soldiers on duty the previous evening.

Our spirits lifted and by nightfall we were rounding the headland next to Bessy's Cove. Gratefully, the men tied off the lugger and walked up the steeply shelving beach, glad to be back on good Cornish soil.

The sound of a flint striking reached my ears and a small illumination caught my eye as the smell of tobacco smoke wafted towards me on the gentle breeze. The stranger had got much nearer to us than I would have thought possible. Whoever he was, he knew how to walk softly.

"What do 'ee want, friend?" said Harry, carefully, one hand on his borrowed pistol.

"Mr Harry Carter," said the strange, perfumed voice, "I come with an important message – from the King."

CHAPTER 3

The two kings

Frederick the Great was certainly a most remarkable man, if he did not possess all the qualities that the world loves to attribute to greatness.

Thomas Babington Macaulay

Harry stared at the man who had made this strange announcement.

"I don't know 'ee, friend," said Harry, "So why would my brother choose to send a message with you?"

It was the stranger's turn to look surprised. Then a look of disgust crossed his face and he replied with a sneer, "I'm not talking of your criminal brother, the so called Smuggler King, the King of your little Prussia Cove; it is an insult to royalty that your brother names himself after a real king, Frederick the Second of Prussia – Frederick the Great." His voice rang with contempt.

"I speak of his Royal Majesty, King George III by the Grace of God, King of this Realm and of His other Realms and Territories, Defender of the True Faith."

It was Harry's turn to look baffled. "You've got a message for me from the King of England?"

The stranger shook his head wearily, but his face still wore a sneer, "I do find it wondrous that such wit and cleverness exists in the world. Yes, your King, the King of England commands your obedience."

The stranger seemed amused that Harry was having such a hard time taking it all in. "When you're ready, Mr Carter, we can talk business... in private." He pointed to a rocky platform some distance from Harry's men. Harry followed meekly. And so did I.

"Mr Carter," began the stranger, "you and your brother are notorious smugglers..."

"We're honest businessmen..." began Harry, but the stranger continued as if he hadn't heard.

"...who have eluded the King's Customs and Excise men for too long. It is time to pay your dues. We are not interested in your petty thieving, but it has come to our attention that you might be... useful to our cause. As you know, the villainous colonials of His Majesty's territories in America have declared themselves a republic..." (here, he spat delicately), "and to our great distress, it seems as if the French will go the same way. We do not," he said angrily, "approve of the guillotine or of republics." He spat again. "We may soon again be at war with our old enemies the French."

"We've been fighting the French on and off for hundreds of years," said Harry, "I don't see that one war more or less will make much difference."

"Then 'tis well that it is I who am charged with our country's defence and not you," said the stranger. "And the difference will be great... very great indeed!" His cold eyes sparkled with fervour and I noticed that his hands shook ever so slightly.

The stranger made a visible effort to control himself. "It has come to our attention," he went on, "that you have certain... abilities to slip between the English coast, the islands of Scilly and mainland France. We believe this... ability... could be of great use to us."

"And how much will you pay me for my… abilities?" said Harry, coolly.

"Pay you? PAY YOU!" shouted the man, losing all control. "You will do it for the honour of serving your King… and if you don't, you will find the attention of His Majesty's Royal Navy more than usually irksome in the coming months. Very irksome indeed. Do you understand me?"

I thought Harry was going to argue with the man, or shoot him with his pistol, but to my surprise Harry nodded his head once. "I understand," he said.

"Good," said the stranger, regaining his genteel poise. "Then you will take these papers, which you will not read, to this address in London. Wait there and someone will come to you."

"London!" said Harry, startled. "You said you wanted me to go to France, but you never mentioned London."

"You have your orders," said the man, disdainfully. "You will obey."

And that's how come me and Harry set off to the big city.

———❦———

In those days only rich people travelled to London. Most people in Cornwall lived their whole lives without ever seeing their capital city. Indeed, there were some as wouldn't admit that London was their capital, and thought of Cornwall as a separate country. Most people spoke English now but one or two of the older folk spoke the singsong language of Old Cornish.

Harry had never been further than the Tamar before. He halted Jethro at the banks of that great river and stared across it. "There lies England," he said, "and there lies our path."

We were the only traffic on the narrow, granite bridge, so no-one saw us pass. Our first night in England was spent in a run-down tavern in the Devonshire village of Gulworthy. I was pretty tired, even though Jethro had done most of the walking. He didn't seem very happy at being stabled with foreign horses and he whinnied when Harry went to leave.

"Now, now, boy," said Harry. "Eat your oats and get your sleep for we've a long journey ahead of us." He stroked Jethro's nose and patted his flanks. I was very glad that Harry didn't make me sleep in the stable, but he popped me inside his coat and I was just as snug as a bug.

It wasn't until later that I found out why Harry kept his coat on in the tavern. When he finally had his fill of meat and ale (with which I shared in full), he undressed in a small, shabby room and I saw that he carried both his pistol and his cutlass with him. They must be violent people, the English, I thought.

But we slept well enough, except for a few bed lice that made me scratch and Harry curse. Jethro looked pleased to see us the next morning and I confess that I was pleased to see him, too.

The people of Devonshsire were a surly, unfriendly lot and I was glad to be done with them when we crossed the county border and Harry told me we were in Somersetshire. Here the people were apple-cheeked and rosy and several farmers' wives stopped us to pass the time of day and to hear the news. I don't think they'd ever met anyone from as far afield as Cornwall before and were curious as to the nature of Harry's journey.

"It's a legal case over an inheritance of land," said Harry with a lie in his teeth and a smile on his face. And the wives would nod and agree that the law was a fool and wished him luck. Once or twice they made us up a parcel of food, so we ate very well, although the strong, sweet ale that they drank, called cider, was not to my taste.

I was becoming accustomed to the road and began to enjoy the novelty of seeing strange places and stranger people. Once we had to get off the road as a large coach drawn by four proud horses went galloping by.

"One day I'll have a coach like that," said Harry, wistfully, "and folk will have to get off the road when I pass and they'll say, 'There goes Harry Carter, gentleman'."

The halfway point of our long journey was in the county of Wiltshire. Sometimes Harry avoided large towns and he decided that the city of Salisbury would hold too many temptations for a country boy, so we headed north of that great place and made our way through open countryside.

Jethro paused in mid step as we rose to the top of a gentle hill and I could fully see why. The three of us stood there with our mouths hanging down around our chins. In front of us in the valley stood a massive circle of stone. It was larger than any building I had ever seen, but had a forlorn air about it as if it had not been loved in a long time. Huge stone pillars stretched into the sky, although several had fallen down and lay quiet in the long grass.

Harry removed his hat and scratched his head, "What is this place?"

But the wind didn't answer him. We walked silently and reverently around the giant ring of stone. Each upright was some three or four times Harry's height and about a hundred times taller than I. It was beautiful but it scared me slightly. It had the solemnity of a church and even Jethro was careful to pick up his hooves quietly.

After an hour of wandering among the great stones, we were no wiser as to the name or purpose of the place, but a picture of it stayed in my mind long after it had faded from sight.

The further East we travelled, the busier became the roads and villages through which we cautiously passed. We were all so used to stepping off the road as another great carriage rolled past, that Jethro automatically moved aside as he heard them coming up behind him.

I noticed that Harry was becoming increasingly nervous. He eyed every stranger from a distance before approaching and at all times kept one hand in the pocket where he carried his pistol and the packet of letters. It was hard to say what he was looking for, but I decided that if he felt the need to be wary, then it was my job to be doubly so. I am normally of a sweet, sunny disposition, friendly to every man and beast who is friendly to me; but I waived my natural gentleness and growled at every man who approached, showing my needle-sharp baby teeth at every opportunity.

At night, Harry refused to sleep in any tavern, but would purchase his meal and carry it off to some lonely spot where the footstep of an intruder could be the more easily heard. Jethro didn't think much of this and looked sullen and hung his head. But I was used to sleeping rough and preferred to be in the fresh outdoors than in some foul-smelling, flea-infested drinking establishment. Besides, I was wrapped up warm inside Harry's greatcoat, so I had nothing of which to complain. As far as I was concerned, we were on an adventure and life was good.

We travelled thus for another few days before I could smell the wood smoke of a thousand fires that signalled we had finally reached the great city.

Have you ever been to London? I had not dreamed that men could build such tall and wonderful buildings. But the beauty of the great, white, shining palaces, money houses and shops were surrounded by the most ghastly hovels of poverty and suffering that it has been my ill luck to see. Children and babies of all ages played in the stinking lanes that overflowed with rubbish and sewage and led down to the oozing muddy banks of a great river; or it would have been a great river had not the waters been the colour and odour of a cesspool. You would not find animals living amongst such filth… excepting the rats, of which there were many.

The children's bare feet and ragged clothes drew Harry's sympathy and he gave away handfuls of coins, but he soon learned that there were more ragged, starving children than there were coins – in the whole world, I think. He had tears in his eyes that he cuffed away angrily. "What dreadful place is this?" he muttered under his breath. When all his small coins were gone, he no longer dared to see the filth and suffering around him, but rode on faster, eyes straight ahead, looking neither left nor right. The children cursed him as we passed and several spat viciously.

I didn't have the heart to growl at them.

Finally, Harry pulled Jethro to a halt as we entered a confusing helter-skelter of narrow lanes, dark alleys and brooding doorways. He muttered to himself as if trying to remember the instructions of the mysterious stranger all those days ago. He shook his head as if to clear it, but I could sense that he was lost.

A small, pale-faced urchin peered up at him. "Spare a penny, Captain?" he said.

"You can have two," said Harry, "if you show me the way to Drury Lane."

"It's a long way, Captain," said the boy, thoughtfully. "I'll show you for three pennies."

Harry weighed up the child's words. "Go on then, boy," he

29

replied.

The child grabbed Jethro's halter and pulled him towards a dingy opening. I didn't like the look of it and without further thought my hackles rose, ready for danger.

The child dragged us through the alleyway until we stumbled, blinking, into the bright sunlight of a broad avenue.

"Drury Lane!" announced the child, with a flourish.

Harry's face was fiery red. "But you said 'twas a long way!" he spluttered.

"I'm sure it's a long way from somewhere, Captain," said the child, cheekily. "You promised me three pennies, Captain."

Suddenly Harry laughed. "I've been well and truly trumped!" he said. "Very well, boy. You have earned your three pennies for making me laugh in this stinking place."

He produced three fat pennies from his purse and handed them to the child.

The pennies were snatched immediately and hidden in the child's ragged clothing. He threw a hasty salute to Harry. "If you need anything else, Captain," said the boy, "just holler for Tomkin, and I'll be there."

"Right you are, Tomkin," replied Harry and waved him off with a smile.

⟹◈⟸

It seemed we had come to the end of our journey. Harry took a room in a small boarding house and Jethro was stabled with several scraggy city horses. But despite his misgivings, I think he was glad of the rest for his hooves had been slipping and sliding on the hard London cobbles and once he almost fell to his knees. Jethro was a country horse, more used to muddy tracks than hard paved streets. His poor hooves ached. He wasn't pleased to be here, and nor was I for London was a filthy place and the people as hard as flint. On our first day I saw a man in fine cloth with a powdered wig step over the body of a dead child with an expression of annoyance. He cared no more for the life of that child than I did for the fleas that now plagued me daily. All three of us were flea-ridden; Jethro whisked his tail in frustration and I sat and scratched and scratched and scratched. Harry took to smoking a pipe as if he hoped to smoke out those tiny fellow travellers.

Tomkin came to see us and each day took Harry and me to a new place of awe and wonder. We stared at the wonderful white palace called the Queen's House. It had once belonged to the great Buckingham family but was now a royal palace. I thought it odd that the Queen lived there by herself. If I lived in such a great palace I'd rather share it with my friends. I thought she must be a very lonely lady.

Tomkin also took us to the pleasure gardens at Vauxhall and advised Harry to keep a close hold on his purse. "I wouldn't rob you, Captain," he chirruped, "but there's them as ain't so scrupulous as I."

"Indeed, Tomkin," said Harry, smiling. "I shall do as you suggest."

The pleasure gardens were very lively. Everywhere people laughed and drank and danced and strolled among the high box hedges. I didn't like the noise much and ducked my head down into Harry's coat, peering out every now and then when the noise seemed a little less. I longed for the peace and quiet of home, for the sound of the waves on the beach and the gulls in the sky. I longed to be away from this place of noise and dirt.

I could tell that Harry felt the same way, too. He had taken to

31

walking down to the river of an evening and leaning over one of the great bridges that spanned its muddy depths. Sometimes, just now and then, I caught the faintest whiff of salt on the river air and I strained to catch the scent again. Instead the city stench rose up to choke us.

One evening, we had just left our lodgings for a short stroll to the river when I sensed that we were being followed. In general this is no good thing. People that know you either call your name and pass the time of day chatting, or cross over the road and pretend not to see you. When someone follows you without speaking, ten to one it means they're up to no good.

My hackles rose and I growled low in my throat – just loud enough to catch Harry's attention.

"What is it?" said Harry. I looked in the direction of the stranger. Harry locked eyes with the man and was about to speak when the man raised a gloved finger to his lips and then beckoned us to follow him.

The stranger wore a long cloak to cover his clothes but I could tell by his boots that he was a gentleman.

Walking briskly, but not too closely, we followed the stranger for over a mile as he weaved his way in and out of dark alleyways and broad, prosperous lanes. Whoever he was, he had a near familiarity with the great city of London. Finally, the man turned into the side door of a large building. Harry moved cautiously, one hand on his pistol.

The narrow stairs opened out into a large and brightly lit apartment, furnished with a lavish elegance that made me stare. Thick silk carpets covered the floor and light flooded down from a chandelier lit by a hundred candles, and at the end of the room was the largest, most ornate mirror that I could ever wish to see.

The small, neat man seated in a large armchair seemed the least significant thing there. Harry must have thought so, too, because I don't think he had even noticed him amongst the glitter and sparkle of the room.

Our guide sank to the floor in a low bow. "Your Majesty," he breathed, "I have brought him, as you ordered."

Harry jumped and stared at the small man. Gaping like the village idiot, his numbed brain rumbled into action and he bent stiffly into the travesty of a bow, dropping his hat in the process.

I saw the small man twitch away a smile, and I liked him at once.

The small man beckoned to me and I trotted over and licked his hand. He tasted very clean. I sat down and leaned against his leg, happily accepting his gentle hand on my head.

"Your Royal… Majesty… Highness… Lord King… Sir, I…" began Harry, breaking out into a sweat.

The small man spoke quietly. "We thank you for coming, Mr Carter," said the man. "Your King and your country have great need of your services."

"Of course, of course," muttered Harry. "Anything. Anything at all. Just tell me how I can help."

The small man nodded thoughtfully. "We are happy to hear this. You have papers for me? You have not read them?"

"No! I mean, Yes and No," stuttered Harry.

The small man read the papers then waved Harry near and handed him a rolled piece of parchment.

Harry stumbled forward to accept it and clumsily crushed the scroll in his beefy hand. He flushed bright red and began to stutter his apologies.

The small man waved his hand and Harry fell silent.

"This," said the small man, pointing at the scroll, "is your

Letter of Marque. It means you are now one of our Royal men and as such, you are exempted from the interest of our Customs and Excise officers. You may travel from and to these shores with a liberty and legality which you have never, we are sure, presumed to enjoy before this time."

Harry looked dazed.

The small man continued. "You are a smuggler no more, Harry Carter, but a loyal subject of your King. Do you accept this and promise to do your duty and our bidding – the bidding of your King?"

Harry nodded wordlessly and sank to his knees.

"Good," said the small man. "Then we request that you take these papers to France for us," and the cloaked gentleman handed a thick packet of parchment to Harry. "They are our private papers sealed with our mark," continued the small man, "You will not look at them, Mr Carter." Harry nodded his obedience.

"There, at the time and place of our bidding, you will deliver them to one who will make himself known to you by the wearing of a particular ring. It is the exact sister of this."

The small man held forth his soft, white hand and showed Harry a large ring. It had a bright green gem at the centre and was surrounded with shiny, white stones that sparkled in the candlelight. Harry later told me that these were diamonds and very valuable.

"Do you understand our request?"

Harry nodded again and tucked the papers carefully inside his waistcoat pocket.

The small man spoke once more. "Then all is well. If we have need of you again, Harry Carter, we will send for you."

The interview was clearly at an end and I was sorry for it; I liked the man with the soft, gentle hands who smelled so clean. But I had thrown my lot in with Harry, and thus I followed him back down the stairs.

Once we were outside, Harry seemed to breathe again. "Do you know who that was?" he said to me. "That was the King of England! George the Third himself. And he was speaking to me!

Harry Carter! Fancy that!" and he shook his head again as if afraid to believe the evidence of his own eyes and ears.

We were just heading back to our lodgings, when the man with the cloak and gentleman's boots caught up with us.

"Mr Carter," he said in a voice that held a slight accent. "It would be better for everyone if news of this meeting were kept solely to yourself and your brother."

"But what if I get caught by the Customs and Excise boys?" protested Harry. "Can't I show them my Letter of Marque? Can't I show them I'm the King's man? If I don't, they'll arrest me on the spot."

The man looked at Harry thoughtfully. "It would be better for everyone," he said slowly, "if you don't get caught."

And with that, we were dismissed – and on our way home.

CHAPTER 4

Ambushed!

He that hurts a robin will never prosper.

Cornish Proverb

We were but five miles from the smell of London when the first attack came.

A bend in the road had provided the perfect cover for an ambush but my keen ears had picked up the jangle of a horse's harness and the nervous shuffling of hooves. I growled quietly and Harry was instantly on his guard.

"They'll be expecting us to walk into their trap," he said softly, half to himself, "They'll not be expecting us at the gallop. Jethro, old fellow, time to live up to your Godolphin ancestry and run through these bully boys like a hot knife through butter." Jethro twitched back his ears in acknowledgement.

I had never before had the privilege of experiencing Jethro at a full gallop. I think I would have enjoyed watching him more than being in Harry's pocket when Jethro started to run. His easy-going stride broke into a furious gallop and I was thrown around like a cork in a storm.

Jethro hurled us full tilt towards the ambushers; his eyes wide and his nostrils flared. The men scattered before him like May blossom. Two or three managed to get off some wild shots but Harry screamed his war cry and pointed his pistol at the nearest of the ambushers as he hurtled past. A blossom of crimson erupted from the man's chest and with a cry he fell to the ground as dead as a doornail.

Jethro must have galloped for a full mile after that until Harry gradually slowed him to a standstill, his flanks heaving with the

effort of breathing; a foam of sweat clung to his neck and mane. Harry stroked his nose and with gentle care calmed the great warrior horse we called Jethro.

"Well done, old fellow," said Harry as he stroked Jethro's nose. "Well done."

We walked for some miles to allow Jethro to cool down and recover his breath and I was doubly glad to feel the road beneath me. There was no doubt that Jethro could carry me along at a great rate, but I confess I preferred my own four paws; humans seemed designed to sit astride a horse but it was not for one such as I. But never again would I think that a horse was a stupid creature. That day Jethro showed me the courage and valour that lived inside his noble heart. I was humbled.

After that, we travelled only during the brief hours of dawn or dusk, or, when the moon was bright enough to light our road. We saw the world in greys and blacks and the occasional silvery white when the moon slipped briefly from behind a cloud. Harry became increasingly furious at the slow pace of our journey and cursed the path that had taken him on this venture to London and back again.

We all longed to glimpse the sea from some lofty cliff, smell the salt on the air and heed the cry of the gulls. Harry was also worried about the state of the family business and the increased strain it would put on John. "Damn it!" he swore, one day. "Will this road never end?"

I knew how he felt.

We had been on the road many days by this time and we were wearied of travel and travail. The constant vigilance had worn Harry's resolution very thin and I confess that I was not immune to the periods of gloom that had begun to assail him. When I sensed the clouds gathering, I licked his hand for comfort, and Harry would look down and a hint of a smile would cross his gaunt face.

Heroic Jethro dragged his tired hooves one weary pace after another and plodded on across the land. The vibrant harvest countryside we had crossed on our way to London was now seen in the muted greys of night. The owls and stars were our only companions.

But one happy day we ascended the gentle, rolling hill that looked down on the mighty Tamar River below us.

"Across there lies Cornwall and home," sighed Harry. "Four more nights and we'll be in our own beds again!"

Jethro shook his mane and neighed happily. I bounced around on Harry's saddle, then scrambled down and chased my tail from sheer joy. I was delighted to hear Harry laugh out loud. I had grown considerably during the last weeks and it was a sad day when I was no longer the little pup who could fit snugly into Harry's pocket. Strangely, this didn't make it easier to catch my tail when I chased it. I would have thought it should have, as my legs were that much longer. Life was a puzzle and no mistake.

After that, we travelled more quickly, and by day, Harry feeling safer now that he was back in his homeland of Cornwall.

The second attack took us almost completely by surprise.

Since a pup, I had associated the vivid smell of wild garlic with home. It grew freely among the hedgerows around the castle of my birth. It had a sweet, pungent smell and my brothers, sisters and I had frolicked in it – much to the annoyance of our ever patient mother.

I recognised the scent of garlic at once. But this was a much stronger smell and mixed with the sweat of a number of unwashed men – men who were hiding. I barked urgently. It was almost too late; the men were upon us. Jethro reared in fury and fear, flailing with his iron-shod hooves. The sudden movement unhorsed Harry, who crashed to the ground, winded.

Determined to do my duty, I sank my teeth into the first plump calf that presented itself nearest to Harry. I was rewarded with a shriek and some cursing in a tongue I did not recognise.

Jethro, still kicking and bearing his teeth, prevented the ambushers from getting their hands on Harry or his precious papers.

"C'est lui! Tirez le cheval!" shouted one of the ambushers and an ugly, scar-faced man levelled a pistol at Jethro and pulled the trigger.

Jethro whinnied in pain as the bullet passed through his left ear. The ambusher had made a mistake. Maddened by the shot, Jethro launched himself at his assailant, trampling the evil creature into the ground; the other ambushers scattered before his wrath. I joined in, barking wildly and biting at any piece of exposed flesh I could reach.

By this time, Harry had recovered his breath and managed to get off a shot from his pistol. The ambushers' resolution shattered, they ran like the dirty humans they were. The smell of garlic and sweat receded with them and from that moment till this day, I can smell a Frenchie at a thousand paces.

I could tell that this second attack had worried Harry far more than the first, but not because the ambushers had come more nearly to a successful conclusion of their vile business, or that they were foreigners and Frenchies to boot, but because they had known where we'd be.

"They knew me," he said, frowning. "They knew where I'd be. Then they must surely know where I live – where my family

41

live. How can I protect them if I have to travel to France? Perhaps I can only protect them by travelling to France, by leaving the country. Will they be safer if I am gone far from these shores with these damnable secret papers? Will I? Will they?"

That evening, worried and worn, we reached Harry's home. With a cry of delight he fell into his brother's arms. "Thanks be to God!" murmured John. "We had all but given 'ee up, brother mine. God has brought you home safe and well. Now sit and take a breath and a dish o' tay."

Gratefully, Harry sank into a deep chair as Tom bustled Jethro off to the stable, promising him the best oats and a bucket of beef tea.

I sprawled out in front of the fire, happily accepting the caresses of the girls Jenna and Jessie.

Harry took a long draught of tea and explained his mission and our adventures up to the moment we'd arrived back at Prussia Cove.

"… and so," said Harry, "I must tek these damnable papers to France. The sooner the better."

"I don't see that there's any such cause for rush," said Meg, putting aside her knitting. "I'm sure the King of England could have sent the papers much faster by some other method than you!"

"Tha's true," said Harry, deep in thought. "He could have, indeed – a carriage to Dover and a fast ship to Calais. But that's not what concerns me now. These Frenchies know where I live. You're all in danger while I remain here. The sooner I go, the better." And with that he sighed heavily.

In the firelight, brother John's face seemed more gaunt and hollow-eyed than usual. "They'll not attack us here," he said, grimly. "We're too well defended; they'd be fools to try."

"I'm not afraid of a full on attack," said Harry. "No. I doubt they've the men nor the courage to try such a thing. But I am afraid of a cowardly attack – an ambush. Suppose they targeted the girls, or Tom or Meg. No, I must leave, and leave quickly."

Meg looked horrified at the prospect of anyone hurting her darling children and threw a harsh look at Harry that I thought was not at all kind.

John simply asked, "What do you need?"

"A fast boat," said Harry. "I'll take the Zennor Mermaid. She'll fair fly through the water."

John nodded his head. "You'll need another man to help sail her." Then he looked at his wife, "…so you'd best be packing my things, Meg."

"NO!" shouted Meg and Harry together.

"No!" said Harry, again. "You're needed here, John. You've a wife and family to look after and a business to run – I'll not be the man that separates you from either!"

I could see that John was not pleased with the idea and the family argument rumbled on into the night. But I was warm and safe and full of sausages and so I fell into a deep and dream-free sleep.

The day I left home for France dawned bright and clear with a pleasing offshore breeze. I felt almost happy to be off on another adventure. I didn't really mind where I went so long as Harry were by my side.

I had counted without the terrible seasickness that beset me before we had sailed beyond sight of land.

I lay whimpering in the bottom of the boat as my stomach rolled and pitched, every now and them squirting a vile tasting bile into my throat.

Harry looked at me with sympathy and gave some kind words.

"You're feeling a smidgeon nashed, for sure, little maid, but 'twill pass in a few hours, I promise 'ee."

The thought of feeling so ill for hours to come made me wretched indeed.

But Harry was right, and by that evening I was feeling enough like myself to join them in a meal of bread and the salted pilchards that Meg had thoughtfully provided. I began to enjoy the wind in my face and the speed at which we flew across the sea to France.

On the second day we sighted a distant sail. Harry unwrapped the waxed cloth that protected his precious brass telescope from the salty air and leant on the boat's rail to steady his arm and take careful sight.

"'Tis George Pengilly and his boys out of Perranporth," he said. "They must be chasing the pilchards, though 'tis late in the season."

We hove to, and waited for the Pengillys to approach.

As the newcomers drew up, Harry yelled, "What news, boys?"

"A fair catch of pilchards, Harry," said George Pengilly, "but we had to turn back early because there's far too many Frenchies for us and we thought we'd spied a Barbary pirate vessel yesterday evening. They're getting bolder and bolder. I'd almost hoped for the boys from the Royal Navy to come around and send 'em packing, although I suspect you'd not wish 'em to interrupt your own business as such." And they sailed off laughing, towards the northeast, towards Cornwall.

Harry watched them wistfully. "I'd not mind 'em Navy boys right now," he muttered, "whatever George Pengilly thinks."

After that, Harry constantly took sightings with his telescope, straining his eyes to catch sight of an enemy sail. He knew we could not outrun a French warship or a Barbary pirate once we had been seen.

As is often the case with the business of smuggling, whether it be brandy or papers from the King, I find it is best not to be seen at all.

CHAPTER 5

Pirates!

We have been forced to draw carts of lead with ropes about our shoulders and have carried great bars of iron. I believe all Christian people have forgotten us in England, because they have not sent us any relief since we have been in slavery.

John Willdon, British slave
from *White Gold*, Giles Milton

Our luck ran out just before dawn two days after we had set sail.

At this time the slave trade was a thriving business and many a son and daughter of Cornwall had been sold into captivity, to die in shackles under a foreign sun. The Barbary pirates sailed from the port of Salé on the North African coast, terrorising small villages and fishermen along every coastal part of Europe and even the Americas.

Cornwall had suffered terribly from these attacks and over the last few years Harry had lost many a friend for good to the 'White Gold' trade in European slaves. Whole villages had been emptied and on one occasion the pirates had even come ashore at St Michael's Mount whilst the villagers were at their Sunday worship. Sixty men, women and children had been dragged from the church and taken as slaves onto the pirate's ship never to be seen again. Mounts Bay was but three miles from Harry's home at Prussia Cove.

So when Harry saw a strange sail on the horizon at sunset, he feared the worst.

"There's nary a ship that I know of as has sails such as these," he said to me with a worried expression on his face. "I fear 'tis pirates from the Barbary Coast, Corsairs out of Salé."

Harry hoped that the ship would pass us in the night and we would be safe. But it was not to be.

At dawn, the sail was still to be seen on the horizon – as was ours. Within the hour it became clear that the pirates had seen our sail and were coming to get us. With all his years at sea and all his skills as a sailor, even Harry could not outrun a Corsair ship with a little fishing skiff such as ours.

Harry made the only preparations he could. He opened and read the secret papers entrusted to him by the King of England. He was not a quick reader or, by the furrows in his brow, did he find reading easy. But he read each paper many times, memorising as much as he could before wrapping them in waxed paper and hiding them in a secret compartment at the stern of the boat. I cowered beside a coil of rope, ashamed by my lack of fortitude.

By mid morning the pirates had us.

The men had dark skins and handsome, sharp-featured faces, but I do not think that I saw an ounce of pity in their souls. They wore long, flowing tunics and decorated themselves with gold chains and earrings; almost all had shaven heads which gave them a sleek, shark-like appearance. Fluttering above their great ship was a green flag, embroidered with the skull of a man. Their intention was clear.

Standing beneath the flag was the one I took to be the captain. He alone wore a bright red silken scarf around his head that I later found out was called a 'turban'. He was the most merciless man I have ever met – I do not think it right to call him a human being, such was the extent of his depravity and enjoyment of cruelty. A pirate is not a romantic figure at all.

"Put down your weapons," called the pirate captain in good English. "Resist and you die."

Harry obeyed mutely as he was dragged aboard and the Zennor Mermaid was secured to the pirates' own ship with thick ropes.

I hoped not to be seen, thinking I might be able to rescue Harry at some later time, but I was soon discovered when two of the pirates boarded our skiff to search for booty.

They yelped in surprise and I growled fiercely, my hackles raised. They shouted something at the captain and by their gestures I could tell that they were asking whether to kill me or throw me overboard. It wasn't much of a choice, but once you're dead, you're dead, so I hoped they would throw me overboard and I would take my chances. I was surprised, therefore, when the largest of the pirates grabbed me by the scruff of the neck and instead threw me onto the deck of the pirate ship.

I ran to Harry and stood trembling at his side.

Harry was staring at the pirate captain. His eyes fair bulged from his head and he shook his head slowly, not believing what he saw.

"I know you," he said, wonderingly. "I know you."

The captain's eyes glittered strangely.

"You're Tommy Pellew's boy, Francis," said Harry in a wondering voice. "We shared a slate together at school. We thought you were dead long ago."

"I was dead," said the pirate captain. "The Francis Pellew you knew died a long time ago. My name is Ahmad bin Khalid. Or Ahmad the Terrible. You choose… Harry Carter."

"Then you do remember me!" said Harry, beginning to smile.

"That was another lifetime, another person," said Ahmad.

"But you're a Cornishman, born and bred," cried Harry.

"It means nothing to me now," was the stern reply.

"Then you've truly turned Turk," said Harry angrily.

"As you see!" snarled Ahmad. He shouted at his men in a foreign tongue and Harry was dragged away.

My spirits were low indeed. From the age of three months

Harry had been my constant companion and friend – now he had been taken from me. I whined piteously, but my misery only earned me hard looks and curses. I soon learned to stay silent and I was allowed to live as long as I was useful.

Those who were not useful or valuable were dealt with harshly. On the second day on board, a sickly prisoner was dragged from the ship's hold and fastened across the front of the pirates' large, brass cannon. His fear was terrible to behold as the pirates taunted him and pretended they were going to fire the cannon. Instead, Ahmad the Terrible chose a lingering death for the poor prisoner. He cut off the man's ears with his dagger and threw him overboard to feed the sharks that soon drew near with the scent of blood. His screams of pain were not as soon ended as I might have hoped; it was some minutes before the man's soul was finally freed from earthly torment and released into eternity. Ahmad laughed aloud during the whole vile affair whilst a deep anger grew inside me at the extent of man's cruelty. Ahmad had truly earned his name, 'the Terrible'.

My job was to catch the rats that plagued the lower decks of the ship. At first I was puzzled as to how so many vermin could be on board whilst we were at sea, but rats are intrepid swimmers and they go from one ship to another when in port, climbing up the anchor chain and lines that tie the ship to the harbour. They also breed extremely quickly!

At first I felt sorry for the poor blind rat babies that infested the ship, but baby rats soon turn into vicious grown up rats; I forced myself to be like the pirates – without mercy. It helped that early on I suffered a most painful rat bite to my cheek which swelled up horribly. There was no Harry to comfort me and I spent several miserable days hoping that I would die. But that wish was not granted, for which I was grateful because in the following days I discovered where Harry was being held.

The lowest part of a ship is an unpleasant place. It is always full of foul seawater, dirt, decay and vermin. There is no daylight and less hope. Here, the pirates kept their prisoners and Harry among them.

One day, I was ratting as usual when I heard a man's voice singing softly. I recognised the melody at once: High Barbaree, a Cornish sea shanty. Harry had often sung it or whistled the tune whilst he worked. I let out a hopeful bark.

There was a pause, and then I heard a voice call out, "Is that you, little maid?"

I barked happily.

"I'm glad to hear 'ee," said Harry, "for I feared the worst. We're in a right caudling here, and no mistake."

After that, I visited Harry whenever I could; it was a great pleasure just to hear his voice, for 'twas the only kind word I would have all day. And I think Harry was pleased to know that I was near.

A dozen other prisoners were held with Harry, although none of them spoke English. There were four Spaniards, two Irish and six Portugee, one of whom was just a little lad of seven or eight. Harry was fond of the little boy who was called Inigo and they whiled away many hours in their dark prison with Harry teaching the child English and learning a few words of Portugee himself. I envied them both at such times for I had not a single companion amongst the pirates – to them I was of small worth, fit only for killing rats. No kind word or comforting pat came my way. I was thrown a bone every couple of days and that was it for me.

As the days wore on, I began to detect a change in the weather. The air grew warm and moist and I could see from the position of the sun that we had travelled a long way south. Two days later we arrived at the port of Salé. If there is a Hell on Earth, then this is the place.

The prisoners were led blinking into the bright African sunlight; their clothes stiff with filth and sea salt. Huge chains were placed about their ankles, so that each man had to drag his feet along the ground. I had not thought that humans could be so cruel to their fellow creatures.

The captain, Ahmad the Terrible watched them dispassionately, oblivious to their mute suffering, blind to Harry's misery. The fact that he was a fellow Cornishman and former schoolmate meant nothing. I perceived that he positively enjoyed the power of life and death that he held over his prisoners.

Poor little Inigo was wailing and crying, such were his terrors. The captain shouted at him but the child was beyond calming by words. Ahmad struck him hard across the cheek and the boy fell to his knees.

"You vile monster!" shouted Harry. "What have you become?"

"Your master," replied Ahmad with a cold smile. "You will do well to remember that."

Harry helped Inigo to his feet as the boy wept silently. I crept along behind the slaves, trying not to be seen. I would follow Harry unto death, if need be.

The dusty market place was a riot of brightly coloured cloth and people from a dozen nations, sweating in the noonday sun; each was there to sell or to purchase a slave. Lives were bought, sold and sometimes ended in that merciless place. Slaves were executed for the crowd's enjoyment.

Over the years, I have heard many people curse my kind: it is not uncommon to hear humans refer to those they despise as a 'dirty dog' or 'vile cur'; but say what you like about my kind – we do not kill each other for pleasure. That is human nature only.

Just a few days earlier, Harry and I had been masters of our own destiny, but no longer. Harry was made to run up and down, dragging his chains, jump and skip, to test his agility. Then he had his jaws forced open to check his teeth and general health. But Harry's humiliation was nothing to the physical beatings to which some slaves were subjected, and he carried his head high.

Inigo attracted much attention, for he was a pretty boy, despite his dirty, tear-spattered face. He was sold to a vastly fat man for £40. Harry begged hard to be sold with the boy, but he was ignored and Inigo was dragged away screaming Harry's name. I never saw him again.

Being fit and strong, Harry was sold for £55 – a vast sum in those days – and fastened to a cart that carried his new master. I followed at a safe distance, darting through the crowd to avoid capture, as Harry was led in chains from the market.

But luck and hope had not yet abandoned our cause.

Harry's purchaser was a dull fellow, but not unkind. When we had travelled some two miles from the market, he released Harry from his heavy chains, replacing them instead with a thick rope, so although Harry was still bound, he could walk more easily. He fed Harry with pieces of bread and fruit, morsels of which Harry passed secretly to me.

We settled down for the night in comparative comfort. I was happy to curl up once again by Harry's side as he stroked me gently.

Towards dawn, I awoke abruptly, uncertain as to what had

caused my alarm. Harry stirred next to me and I growled softly. The slave owner still snored noisily by the fire.

Two men in long robes stole out of the gloom. Harry knew not whether they were friend or foe. One grabbed the sleeping slave owner who was jerked into wakefulness with a shout and a knife at his throat.

"Who are you?" whispered Harry.

"Are you English?" said the second man.

"No!" replied Harry. "I'm a Cornishman!"

The men grinned. "Well, we're from Devonshire," they said, "but we'll help you all the same," and they made to cut the throat of the slave owner.

"No!" shouted Harry again. "He has not been unkind."

The Devonshire men stared at him. "You've not been a slave long as long as us, I think," said the first, "or you would desire his death."

"I desire no man's death," said Harry, "except one… and he is Francis Pellew – or Ahmad the Terrible as he now calls himself."

"Very well," said the first Devonshire man, nodding slowly. "We will not kill this Turk, but you had better take his robes to disguise yourself."

They explained their plan of escape to Harry.

"We hope to smuggle ourselves onboard a ship at Salé that is going to Portugal. From there it will be easy to get a passage home to Plymouth."

Harry smiled. "It's a plan, but I have another. My own ship, the Zennor Mermaid, a smart little skiff, has been taken to Salé. We take her back and sail to Gibraltar. We can be there in two tides, and safe from these monsters."

And so we retraced our steps to Salé.

Our new companions gave their names as Walter Abbot from

Honiton and William Addiscott from Exmouth. Both had been mariners out of Plymouth when captured some six years previously. Both spoke Turk well enough to aid our disguise and subsequent escape.

The market was already busy when we arrived an hour after dawn. Will and Walter chattered away in the local tongue and Harry pretended to listen, nodding and shaking his head at intervals. Their disguise was perfect except for one detail – me.

I do not wish to boast and am not much given to vanity, but although I am small, I am rather noticeable, being thought a pretty maid.

In a seemingly casual manner, we approached the dock where the Zennor Mermaid was moored.

"There she is," whispered Harry under his breath.

"Well, well," said an amused voice. "'Tis Harry Carter's dog… and Harry Carter, too."

We turned in horror. It was Ahmad the Terrible, with his dagger drawn.

I launched myself at the vile creature and sank my teeth into his sword arm. No longer a puppy, my teeth were sharp and strong and I did not let go.

Ahmad howled in pain and several people in the crowd looked round; many of them wore amused expressions to see the torturer tortured thus.

Ahmad thrashed around trying to release me and in doing so, knocked over a stall selling coloured silks. The trader's howl of anguish as his precious merchandise lay in the dusty streets was nothing to his fury as young boys dodged out of the crowd to steal his wares.

Soldiers ran to the scene adding their voices to the din. In that press of human flesh, nobody noticed our small party. Harry grabbed Ahmad and forced his arms behind his back and I thankfully let go. Walter pushed his sun-darkened visage into Ahmad's face.

"You stinking traitor," he said. "You don't deserve to speak the King's English," and with that he drew Ahmad's own dagger as if to slice off his tongue.

"No!" said Harry. "We must not sink to his level!"

Walter hesitated then slammed the base of the dagger into Ahmad's skull, stunning him and sending him into unconsciousness.

Without speaking we hurriedly made our way to the Zennor Mermaid. The noise and confusion had rendered us invisible to our former captors and we had no trouble sailing away from that place.

I was not certain whether I was glad or sad that Harry had chosen to save Ahmad's life: it is a terrible thing to wish the death of another living creature, but so evil a man was he, that I feared for any creature who crossed his path. But as neither Walter nor William gave the matter a second thought and instead expressed their joy at being free men once again, I let the matter rest.

They laughingly abused Harry for his soft heart. It was this I loved most about Harry and so I pitied men such as Ahmad who had too much hate in their own hearts.

The wind stayed fair and within a day we had made our way safely into the English-ruled port of Gibraltar. We were sorry to see the cheerful Devonshire men leave and I think they were sorry to say their farewells, too. But our way lay to France and they longed to return to their native lands. Harry wished them well and, recovering his stash of gold coins from the boat's secret hiding place, he pressed a sovereign into each of their hands and saluted them as brothers.

I know not what became of William and Walter but I hope they reached their homeland once more.

The King's papers were still in their hiding place. Harry looked at them sadly, knowing that his duty took him to France instead of home. And so Harry replenished our provisions for the journey ahead, securing a large and tasty bone for me.

With joy and sorrow combined in our hearts, we sailed north along the Portuguese coast, then headed across the Bay of Biscay, making landfall a short distance from the busy coastal town of Brest.

CHAPTER 6

Liberté, Egalité, Fraternité

Revolutions are usually accompanied by a considerable effusion of blood, but are accounted worth it – this appraisement being made by beneficiaries whose blood had not the mischance to be shed.

Ambrose Bierce

Harry eased the Mermaid into a narrow inlet of Cape Finistère on the French coast. It was a wild and rocky place, not unlike our own Land's End. Harry called the place 'Brittany' and I thought it odd that a place in France should be called after 'Britain' but supposed it natural that they would rather be British than French – although calling a person such does not make it so. I should like to be as tall as a wolfhound, but calling me 'wolf' will not add to my height.

We nighted there, as cosy as fleas in a wig. Harry's instructions were to round the Cape as near to Brest as he dare, then make the final journey to that town on foot. At the sign of the Coq au Vin, he was to wait in the tavern for the man with the diamond and emerald ring to approach him.

"It doesn't seem like much of a plan," said Harry; not unreasonably, I thought.

The truth was, he had been in too much awe of the King to question these instructions, but in the cold light of day, they seemed flimsy indeed.

"How will the man know that I've arrived?" he muttered. "I'm some weeks later than expected."

We set off on foot for Brest for what I hoped would be the final leg of our adventure.

I was, by now, a seasoned and worldly traveller, but I sorely wished for Jethro's comforting presence and broad saddle. Every now and then Harry took pity on my short, young legs and carried me over his shoulder as if I weighed no more than a feather.

As with all places where many humans gather, I smelled Brest before I could see it. We had garnered many a glance on our short journey; Harry's clothes marked him as a stranger, and although he spoke some French, his accent marked him as a foreigner. But the Frenchies we met were generally welcoming and not so hostile as they that had ambushed us back home in Cornwall. I knew by now that the world is a far more complicated place than I had imagined. Not all Frenchies were evil and, sadly, not all Cornishmen were kind and trustworthy.

With Harry's halting French, we easily found the Coq au Vin tavern and settled into a snug alcove with a jug of wine, a smelly cheese and a large platter of garlic sausages. I soon understood why so many Frenchies smelled of garlic – the sausages were delicious indeed, melting on the tongue and warming the stomach. They did have an unfortunate side effect later on and Harry, who is normally glad to have me sleep by his side, pushed me from the bed and told me to sleep in the corner.

Three days we waited at the Coq au Vin. Harry wouldn't let me eat any more garlic sausages, for which I was very sorry, but I made do with lamb, mutton and beefsteaks instead. I made friends with many people at the tavern who had, as it turned out, a soft spot for a youngster such as I. Indeed, I ate so many titbits from people's leftovers that my stomach began to resemble a small football. I was very happy. Harry had taken the precaution of hiding the King's papers in the waxed bag and placing them in the old water trough at the back of the stables. Which was just as well, because that evening, they came for him – and 'twas not the man with the emerald and diamond ring.

Twenty armed soldiers swept into the tavern and took Harry at gunpoint. He put up no resistance for to have done so would have meant instant death. The tavern owner held me tight and I was unable to run to Harry's aid. I do not know what good I could have done, I just knew that I wanted to help him. But the tavern owner had been most kindly to me and I was loath to bite him. So I wriggled and kicked but to no avail. The men took Harry, tied his wrists and marched him away. Not a word had been spoken.

As the soldiers left, the tavern owner relaxed and I leapt from his arms, landing with a soft thud on the straw-covered floor. I scampered after the retreating soldiers, but soon fell behind as their well-fed horses galloped out of sight.

A feeling of dread crept through me, but I kept my head and followed at a distance, the soldiers' scent being clear and fresh and easy to follow.

They did not take Harry far, but my heart sank when I saw the enormous stone castle into which they dragged him. I did not think things could get much worse. I was alone again.

Two vast, round, windowless towers stood guard on a narrow entranceway that was further defended by a fearsome-looking portcullis. But you know, the funny thing about human prisons is that they're rarely built to keep out one such as I.

I had learned from Harry that if you want to look like you belong, you have to act like you belong. I simply walked through the castle's entrance – the same one through which

Harry had been dragged as a prisoner.

Beyond the portcullis was a large, sunlit courtyard. I heard Harry's voice at once. He was shouting, but he sounded more annoyed than afraid.

"I told you," he bellowed, "I don't speak Frenchie."

I followed Harry's voice up a narrow stairway and was forcibly reminded of my birthplace: the blue-grey granite stairs and spiral staircase were just as I remembered from my earliest days at Pengersick Castle. I thought of my poor mother and 10 brothers and sisters for the first time in many weeks.

But I didn't have time for fond reminiscences – I had to rescue Harry. So I trotted up the stairs towards the sound of his voice.

To my surprise, Harry was sitting at a large wooden table in a well-furnished, sunny room. He didn't appear to be tied to the chair and, on the contrary, had been provided with food and drink in quantity. He was loosely guarded by two young soldiers who were barely out of boyhood, one of whom appeared to have been trying to engage Harry in conversation. The homely picture provided such a surprising contrast with his rough capture, that for a moment I paused unmoving at the door.

Then Harry saw me, and his shout of delight made the two soldiers jump. I ran to him and he scooped me up in a tight hug that made me squirm.

"Little maid!" he said in wonder, "You really are the cleverest beastie that ever there was. How did you find me here?"

I licked Harry's hand affectionately and was happy to help him finish the plate of lamb, gravy and white bread that he had been eating.

The youngest of the two soldiers came over to stroke me and chattered away companionably in French to both me and Harry.

I quickly revised my thoughts about the French and decided that some of them were nearly as nice as Cornish people – and a lot nicer than one Cornish person in particular of whom I dislike to think.

It's a funny thing: here we were, at war with the Frenchies, and they were treating us like long lost friends. And Harry's long lost friend, Ahmad the Terrible, had treated us like we were enemies at war. It was a puzzler and no mistake.

Both soldiers snapped to attention when a senior officer entered the room. He dismissed them abruptly and closed the door behind them.

I was astonished to recognise the newcomer: it was the gentleman whom we had first met in London – the one with the expensive boots – who had taken us to meet the King of England.

Harry was about to speak when the man waved him to silence.

"You're late," he said.

Harry bristled with indignation and gave a rapid account of our adventures with the Barbary pirates.

The man raised his eyebrows at the description of our escape, but made no comment. "The papers," he said, "the papers you were given by the King of England – are they safe?"

"Yes," said Harry, "they're safe. But…" he admitted slowly, "I have read them…"

"What?!" thundered the man. "How dare you? You were explicitly told not to read them!"

"Aye," said Harry, "but I thought 'twere best to memorise 'em in case I were parted from 'em for good. As luck may have it, they are safe."

"Very well," said the man dismissively. "It is now imperative that we take the papers to Paris at once."

"I thought I were supposed to wait for the man with the diamond and emerald ring," said Harry, puzzled.

"Yes, you were," replied the man shortly, "but he couldn't wait for you – for your unfortunate detour. We must leave for Paris tonight."

Harry nodded curtly. "Then if we are to be travelling together," he said, "I should like to know your name, sir."

"I have the honour to name myself Pierre August Robert Boniface, Le Conte de Faucigny-Lucinge et Coligny."

Harry's eyes watered at the thought of remembering half such a name. I am very glad that my name is short and sweet – everyone remembers 'Pip', which is very important at meal times.

For the first time the man smiled briefly. "You may call me Pierre when we are alone," he said, "or simply 'sir' when anyone else is around. In this new age of revolution it does not do to be a member of the aristocracy. To the soldiers I command, I am Citizen Coligny."

Our mode of transportation was quite different from anything that I had previously experienced: we travelled by coach.

Harry nearly swooned when he saw the luxurious padded leather and wide, comfortable seats. I was impressed against my will, for I did not want to admit that the French might have something better than us Cornish. But few carts and fewer carriages were seen in Cornwall in those days owing to our rough and narrow roads. I had heard Harry talk enviously of one gentleman of the St Aubyn family who lived in Falmouth, who had his own carriage, but no-one that we knew had ever travelled in such luxury.

The carriage was pulled by four high spirited grey horses, but they weren't as friendly as Jethro when I went up to introduce myself. They merely nodded disdainfully and blew their nostrils at me. Now I happen to think that blowing your nostrils at someone is very rude indeed and not at all how my mother brought me up, so I ignored the ill-behaved brutes and bounded into the carriage to sit in dignified silence.

Harry climbed in slowly behind me. "Harry Carter," he whispered to himself, "You be travelling like a gentleman after all!"

We changed horses twice during the night, and, by dawn, we were approaching the city of Rennes.

Pierre insisted that we pull down the blinds on the carriage windows.

"It will be best," said Pierre, "if as few people as possible know we are on the road. Word travels fast in these small towns – peasants are such curious people."

Harry frowned at this comment, but held his tongue; he did not like to hear the common people described thus. To Harry, they as worked for a living demanded respect, no matter what their position in life. He could not abide idlers or shirkers but nor could he abide the scent-sniffing upper classes who looked down on the people who ploughed their fields, cooked their food and made their beds.

We breakfasted at Rennes, enjoying being able to leave the carriage to stretch our legs. A small roadside tavern provided us with warm bread straight from the oven, sizzling bacon and various fruits. Pierre also purchased a large garlic sausage and more bread for our luncheon. Harry gave me a hard look for he had not forgotten the effect of garlic sausage on my stomach. I thought I might be able to snatch a small piece when he wasn't looking. Fair is fair.

We travelled thus for two more days, reaching Paris by nightfall on the third day.

Poor, wounded city. The renowned City of Light had become the city of night, and in that night lurked terrors that do not bear repeating.

Small groups of raggedly dressed people were waiting on street corners and stared at us with flinty eyes as we passed. Several hurled stones at the carriage and screamed insults at the windows. Four burly men tried to halt our passage by grabbing hold of the driver's reins but Pierre leaned out of the carriage window and pointed his pistol at the leader's chest.

Whether it was his army uniform or loaded pistol that lent most weight to his argument, I know not, but the men let go of the reins and slunk back into the shadows.

"What's going on?" cried Harry when we were safely moving again.

"Revolution, mon ami," replied Pierre. "The peasants see a carriage and they want to rip it apart; they see an aristocrat and they want to introduce her to Madame Guillotine."

"Who's she?" asked Harry.

"Not 'who' but 'what'," replied Pierre enigmatically. "The guillotine is a 'scientific' way of dispatching people quickly and cleanly."

"What do you mean 'dispatch'?" asked Harry looking worried.

"The guillotine is a machine that cuts off people's heads," replied Pierre, gravely.

At last the carriage pulled up outside an enormous, empty building with a huge studded wooden doorway. But instead of going through this main entrance, Pierre led us around to a small door at the side of the building and knocked three times.

"Oui?" enquired a muffled voice from within.

"I have a package from England," replied Pierre.

The door swung open and we were ushered inside by an elderly man in long, black robes. The light of single a candle illuminated our path as we crept along a narrow passageway, down two flights of stairs and through several empty and echoing chambers.

Finally our guide pointed at another wooden door and gestured for us to knock.

Pierre knocked three times and opened the door which creaked painfully on its ancient hinges. Light flooded out and I stood blinking in the doorway. Harry nearly tripped over me and cursed, rubbing his eyes. Pierre, it seemed, had expected the flood of light for he merely smiled slightly at our predicament.

We stumbled into the room and Pierre closed the door behind us. Our silent guide had vanished into the darkened corridor.

At the far end of the room stood a large throne-like chair. Sitting on it was a short, fat, elderly man. He also wore long, black robes but these were trimmed with purple silk and he wore a broad purple sash around his well-padded waist.

"Father Michael!" said Harry in wonder.

"Yes, my son," said the elderly man. "We meet again. It seems you have gone up in the world – as have I – I am called 'Monsignor' these days."

"Er… is that good?" asked Harry, clearly unfamiliar with the Catholic Church's hierarchy.

The man laughed gently. "Well, it is a promotion of sorts," he replied, "although sadly unappreciated in this godless city, these godless times."

He sighed and I felt sorry for him. I licked his hand in

friendship; the skin was thin and papery. I thought he must be very old indeed. Perhaps he had built the ancient church in which we stood. He patted my head absentmindedly.

"Blimey!" said Harry and then blushed for having sworn in

front of the priest – he was gazing at his hand. "I mean," he stuttered, "it's you! You're the man!"

I saw at once what Harry meant. On the third finger of the man's right hand was a large emerald and diamond ring. The ring was a sister to that which we had seen so many months ago – on the hand of the King of England.

"Ah yes," replied the priest. "I am the one you seek."

"Then these are for you," replied Harry, pulling out the papers that he had been given to deliver and had suffered so much for.

But the priest waved them away, smiling kindly at Harry's dumbfounded expression. "They are not important – it is you that I wanted to see. Do you remember," he continued, "when you saved me from drowning fifteen years ago?"

"Of course I do!" smiled Harry. "Your boat went down off St Michael's Mount and we rowed out to get you."

"Well, I remember it rather more dramatically," said the priest, with raised eyebrows. "Our little boat tore itself apart on the rocks during a fierce storm and you and your brother rowed through ten foot waves to save my boat's crew – you nearly died yourself."

Harry blushed again. "We was glad to do it, Father. 'Twere nothing. We'd have done the same for any poor soul in that tempest."

"Yes, exactly," said the priest, leaning forward to press the point. "And that is why I have asked you here. These are troubled times and I need a man who knows the seas, a man who is not afraid of any save God himself. Will you help me Harry Carter?"

"Of course," said Harry, perplexed. "What can I do?"

The elderly priest didn't answer immediately but sat stroking my head whilst I leaned sleepily against his chair.

"The King of France has been executed," he said, "and they say the Queen will not last many more days. Her children have been taken from her and are imprisoned. Her eldest son, Louis-Charles, the Dauphin, will one day be King in his father's place. But it's not safe for him here in Paris – the prison could be stormed any day and the Dauphin would be taken to the guillotine. He must be taken to England where he will be kept safe until he is old enough to regain his crown. But the revolutionaries watch the ports – they wait for us to make a move. We have one chance to free him; one chance to save his life."

He pointed at Harry. "You, Harry Carter, will provide that one chance; you will be that man."

Harry gasped. "But… but…" he said. "Why me?"

"The plan is to free the boy from prison and take him by rowing boat down the Seine to Honfleur. From there you will row around the coast to Cherbourg where you will find your own boat waiting for you. I've had it sent round by a trusty fellow from Brest; this is a difficult journey fraught with dangerous currents and unpredictable tides."

He paused, peering closely into Harry's face. "And then, Harry, you do what you do best – you smuggle the boy back to Cornwall."

"It's nigh on a hundred miles from Honfleur to Cherbourg!" said Harry. "'Tis a fearsome long way to row!"

"It will be your best disguise," persisted the priest. "The revolutionaries will search all the fast sailing boats, but they will not stop a man and a boy… and his dog."

Harry scratched his beard.

"Right!" said Harry. "Bring me the boy and I'll bring him to

Cornwall."

"Thank you!" said the priest simply. He removed the exquisite ring from his finger and gave it to Harry. "Use this for your passage through England," he said. "When you need to get to His Highness, the King of England, use this as your passport." He leant back as if exhausted.

Harry accepted the ring with a look of wonder on his face. It glinted knowingly in the torchlight.

Pierre, silent all this time, simply nodded in agreement and smiled. I wagged my tail and the bargain was sealed.

CHAPTER 7

A man, a boy, a dog, a boat

In the pauses of our talk, the river, playing round the boat, prattles strange old tales and secrets, sings low the old child's song that it has sung so many thousand years.

Jerome K Jerome, *Three Men in a Boat*

We made our plans carefully.

Harry loaded the little rowing boat with water and provisions for four days. It was a good thing I was there to help because he forgot to pack the garlic sausage that Pierre had so carefully acquired. With some cunning (of which Harry would have been proud had he known what I was doing), I secreted the garlic sausage beneath a small rag of blanket that was to be my bed for the forthcoming journey.

Pleased with my work, I wandered down to the great river with Harry and helped him dig up worms for fishing bait, for Harry and the Dauphin were to be disguised as a father and son out for a day's fishing.

It was such fun digging in the sticky mud on that mild November morning that I near forgot the purpose of our labours, but as the sun sank lower in the sky, a tense excitement filled Harry

The plan was simple, but it depended on courage, timing and luck. I had learnt from Harry that every bold plan is made a good one through luck and we surely needed it tonight.

Six men had been selected by Monsignor Michael to free the

73

Dauphin from his prison. With a combination of bribery, strong wine and some violence, the gaolers would be rendered insensible and the boy would be whisked away on fast horses. Harry and I would be waiting by our boat on the Seine. The tide turned at one hour after midnight, flowing at its fastest back out to sea. If we missed that tide, the Dauphin would be trapped in Paris for another day, with revolutionaries on the look out for any eight-year old boy, no matter how unlikely a prince he seemed.

Pierre was of the rescue party and I could tell that Harry longed to be where the action was at its thickest.

"No, mon ami," said Pierre. "You are the key to this rescue. If anything happens to me, *c'est la vie*, but you must, must succeed."

Harry grasped him by the hand and wished him well.

I, too, was sorry to see him go, for arrogant and proud as he was, he was also courageous, loyal and brave. These are qualities that one does not meet every day – even in Cornwall.

Finally, we bade farewell to Monsignor Michael.

Harry knelt and kissed his hand. Then the Monsignor laid his hand on me as I looked up into his kindly eyes.

"Blessed art thou," he whispered, "and it shall be well with thee."

I saw Monsignor Michael once more as I turned and watched his short, round silhouette fading into the darkening distance.

Harry and I wandered down to the river, acting as if we hadn't a care in the world, when, in reality, every nerve was strained for the slightest noise or cause for alarm.

The Monsignor had decided that Harry should pretend to be a deaf mute, as a way of explaining his lack of French. But the hardest thing was for Harry not to react to sounds.

If anyone has ever stood behind you and suddenly made a loud noise, I would very much doubt that you had failed to jump in alarm. But that was what Harry had to force himself to do. I had to be his eyes and ears and warn in advance of any danger.

We sat huddled together in the little boat as the night grew darker. Although it had been mild during the morning, the day's warmth had long since gone and we could feel the approach of winter in our bones.

As the night progressed I could tell that Harry was worried. The tide had turned and the little boat pulled and tugged at the line tying it to the shore. If the Dauphin did not arrive soon, the night would be lost.

In the distance we heard the sounds of people yelling and the distinctive sound of a pistol firing. We were immediately on our guard and Harry stood up in the boat, his eyes straining to see into the night sky.

I was the first to hear the sound of running feet and growled low in my throat to warn Harry.

He nodded at me and I jumped ashore to see if it were the rescue party or some band of marauding revolutionaries. I immediately recognised Pierre but also caught the scent of blood on the air. Someone had been wounded – and badly.

Pierre saw me at once. His face was pained and blood sheeted his right arm. "C'est la!" he whispered, gesturing towards me with his good arm.

The group of men ran towards us. Hurrying with them was a small, thin, dirty boy, dressed in rags. He looked like the orphan child who lived in the almshouse rather than a prince and king-to-be. The child seemed mute with terror so I licked his hand to show he was amongst friends. He flinched at first, but then clasped me with trembling hands and buried his tear-soaked face in my warm fur.

Pierre whispered instructions in rapid French to the boy who sat wide-eyed and fearful. I could tell that Pierre was worried that the boy had not understood. He repeated his words more urgently, but there was still no response.

He turned desperately to Harry. "I have told the Dauphin," he said, "that he must pretend that you are his father, a deaf mute, and you are out fishing. If anyone asks him, you are a simple fisherman. I hope he has understood."

"We'll manage," said Harry gruffly. "You'd better get your arm seen to, Pierre. It don't look too good."

Pierre smiled faintly and shrugged his one good shoulder. "It is just an arm. I have done my duty. Good luck, mon ami. Travel safely with our little Prince."

Harry raised his hand in farewell and released the line that tied us to the bank. The current snatched the little boat and we were whipped away downstream.

Behind us shouts and shots sounded on the bank but it was too far away to see what was happening and there was nothing we could do. We floated on in silence.

By dawn, we were far from Paris and the child was curled up in the bottom of the boat, wrapped up in Harry's greatcoat, fast asleep.

Dawn's watery light showed his skin to be pale and somewhat sallow – the face of someone who had spent long hours indoors away from the sun. By contrast, Harry's face was as brown as a nut, his hands like tree bark.

The child's eyelids fluttered open, his dark eyes puzzled, then frightened.

"It's all right, son," said Harry gently, "you'll be safe now."

The boy showed no signs of understanding Harry and continued to regard him warily.

Harry passed the boy a hunk of thick black bread and hard cheese that he ate eagerly, sharing odd pieces with me. In trade, I gave him a piece of the garlic sausage I had hidden in my blanket and Harry laughed out loud.

The boy jumped as if he had been shot, then smiled nervously, stroking me all the while.

The tide had turned and was now flooding upstream, so Harry steered the little boat into a bed of reeds that grew thickly at the side of the river. We were well hidden, which was just as well, because shortly after that a barge full of soldiers passed us, using the light wind to sail their way downstream against the current.

There was no doubt that they were looking for the boy. He hid his face in his hands and trembled with fear.

Harry and the boy spent the rest of the day dozing and fishing, waiting for the tide to turn. I sat on guard duty keeping an open eye and two open ears for strangers, but we were left alone.

When the tide turned, we continued with our journey and travelled thus for two more days. Harry talked gently to the boy who began to occasionally murmur 'oui' or 'non', but mostly he sat next to me stroking my fur and playing with my ears. It was very pleasant.

The following evening we reached Honfleur. The river became wider and dirtier and I could smell the salt from the nearby sea. Harry tied up the little boat some distance from the main port.

"Stay here," he said to the boy. "Stay here and I'll come back soon with more food. OK? Stay here."

The boy stared at him blankly and Harry looked worried. "Stay here. Restez ici. Understand?"

Slowly the boy nodded.

Harry turned to me. "Look after him, little maid. I'll be as quick as I can."

I didn't like Harry going in to the town by himself but Harry was a man grown and the boy was just a puppy. I knew where my duty lay.

Two hours passed and I was beginning to worry that Harry had been captured when I heard his steady tread on the riverside path.

"All safe and sound?" he asked.

I wagged my tail furiously and the boy murmured "oui".

"Splendid!" said Harry and handed us each a large slice of a tasty meat pie which was wonderful (although not as good as garlic sausage).

We spent the night on the riverbank, listening to the river rippling past. An hour before dawn, Harry roused us and got out two fishing rods and handed one to the boy.

"If anyone tries to stop us," he said, "tell them we're fishing... and... and that I'm your father, but I'm a deaf mute. Deaf – can't hear, can't talk. Understand? Fishing! We're fishing! Pêche!"

The boy remained silent and Harry looked worried again, but there was no time to waste. Harry untied the boat and we drifted silently down the river, Harry and the boy holding their fishing rods.

We had almost passed the sleeping town of Honfleur when a shout rang out.

"Arretez! Qui est la?"

"Ignore it," hissed Harry.

But the shout rang out again, this time accompanied with the drawing back of a musket's hammer.

Harry was getting ready to duck when the boy cried out, "Il est un sourd-muet! Mon père est un sourd-muet!"

The anticipated shot did not come and we continued to drift down the river whilst a heated debate had broken out between the soldiers on the bank. As their voices faded into the distance Harry began to relax.

"I don't know what you said to them, boy," he said, "but it worked. Well done!"

For the first time the boy smiled.

The next few days were some of the happiest I had known in my short life. The boy began to chatter away in French and Harry taught him a few words of English. Together they sang songs and the boy even took a hand at rowing the boat, although there wasn't much strength in his scrawny frame. But he seemed more like a child again, smiling and even laughing once or twice.

We explored the coast of France as we made our way west towards Cherbourg. Harry knew the coast well from his smuggling exploits and he had many fine tales to tell.

"That's where we had that run in with Rum Barrel O'Connor," he said. "He tried to steal our brandy what we had lawfully bought and paid for and was about to smuggle back to Cornwall. 'Twas a fair old scruff but he came off the worst. Ran off with his tail between his legs – no offence, little maid."

"And that," he said, pointing to a sheer cliff face, "was where we had to lower down ten barrels of tea on a rope. Night was drawing in and I was the last man down; I had to climb that cliff in the dark. Well, I fell the last nine feet and got this scar on my arm for my troubles."

He rolled up his sleeve and showed us a long scar, pale against his tanned skin. Next to it was a blue-inked tattoo of a mermaid.

"Qu'est-ce c'est?" enquired the boy.

"Ah!" said Harry. "That be the Zennor mermaid. I named my boat after her. 'Tis a sad tale indeed."

Harry didn't need much encouragement, for he loved to tell a sad story.

"The village of Zennor is a small, windswept place on the northern part of our coast. The people are poor and earn their living by fishing.

"One of the fishermen was a young fella by the name of Matthew. He was a good-looking boy with the voice of an angel. Matthew sang in the church choir and people came from far and wide to hear him.

"One who heard him was the mermaid Morveren, daughter of the Llyr, king of the ocean. She found his voice so beautiful that she decided she must meet the owner. So she put on her best dress, in the way of humans, and made her way to the church which was not easy, for a fish's tail is not made for walking, and she waited outside the church.

"Well, when Matthew saw her it was love at first sight and he followed her back to her watery home, though his mother cried something fierce.

"Never again were Mathew and Morveren seen by the people of Zennor. They had gone to live in the land of Llyr, in golden sand castles built far below the waters in a blue-green world. Matthew's song was still heard by the people of Zennor, for he sang to Morveren both day and night, love songs and lullabies. When the fishermen of Zennor heard his voice raised in song they knew it was safe to put to sea."

"C'est incroyable!" said the boy, his eyes wide.

As we slowly neared Cherbourg, I knew our happy, carefree days of sea and song would soon be over. Harry became more wary, constantly checking the horizon for unknown sails and, on seeing one, he would hide us in some remote and rocky cove until the danger had passed.

He explained his plan in slow, clear English.

"I shall walk the last ten miles in to Cherbourg. They'll not stop a lone man and you two will be quite safe here until I return with the Zennor Mermaid. You'll be by yourselves over night, but stay hidden until you hear my voice no matter what. Understand?"

The boy nodded his head eagerly and I wagged my tail to show I understood.

"Good," said Harry. "I'll go this evening and hope to be back shortly after dawn, depending on the winds."

The boy and I spent the night huddled together under a thin blanket, praying for Harry's safe and speedy return. As dawn broke, we shared the last of the bread, now rather stale, and turned our eyes west, hoping to catch a glimpse of Harry and the Zennor Mermaid.

The morning dragged by with still no sign of Harry but an hour after midday a sail appeared around the headland. The boy jumped up and down for joy but a cold, leaden feeling weighed in my heart. I did not recognise the sail; it was not the Zennor Mermaid and it was not Harry.

I growled at the newcomer and held onto the boy's leg, trying to pull him back from the shoreline, lest we should be seen. But the boy just shrugged me off and continued to jump up and down and wave. It was one of the few occasions when I wished I were bigger and stronger so I could pull him away.

I tried again, growling and barking and nipping at his ankles. He looked down at me, puzzled, and then I saw fear replace joy on his face. Finally he had understood. We withdrew into the very furthest reaches of the cove, pressing ourselves through a narrow passageway of the smugglers' cave. But there was no way we could hide the rowing boat – all we could do was wait and hope.

As the ship drew nearer, I could hear the voices of the sailors calling to each other in French.

Perhaps they were not soldiers but fishermen, or perhaps they were not looking for so small a vessel as a rowing boat, but whatever the reason, providence was with us and the ship passed by without further incident. It was some minutes before I could persuade the boy to leave the cave and wait once more on the shoreline for Harry.

As the sun sank in the evening, we strained our eyes west in the direction that Harry had disappeared the previous evening. My stomach rumbled uncomfortably and I thought longingly of the garlic sausage that had supplied the first part of the voyage.

As darkness gathered in the east, I finally spied a familiar sail. It was Harry! He had come!

I jumped up and down barking and the boy, at first alarmed, soon joined me in my simple celebrations.

"There you are!" called Harry. "I were afraid I'd miss you in the dark. 'Twas not my plan to be so late but the soldiers are out looking for 'ee."

I wondered why the soldiers might be looking for me but soon realised that it was because I was an important and recognisable part of Harry's team.

It was wonderful to be safe on board the Zennor Mermaid once again, but even better to be homeward bound. I longed to see the green fields and golden beaches of Cornwall.

Harry turned the little skiff around and we headed for home.

CHAPTER 8

Trial by water

And now the storm-blast came, and he
Was tyrannous and strong:
He struck with his o'ertaking wings,
And chased us south along.

Samuel Taylor Coleridge from
The Rhyme of the Ancient Mariner

The morning of the great storm dawned bright and clear but with a blood-red sun that stained the clouds crimson.

"Red in the morning, sailors' warning," said Harry, his eyes restlessly scanning the horizon.

"The storm – will she be very bad, Harry?" asked the boy in a voice that trembled slightly.

"No sailor's ever known a good storm," replied Harry, then seeing the look on the boy's face, "but the Zennor Mermaid is a good little ship – we'll be fine, don't you worry yourself. You just make sure you keep yourself safe. Don't stand up when the storm is blowing for any reason – a little chap like you would be swept overboard in a heartbeat."

I heeded the words, readily believing that they were aimed at me as well as the boy. I didn't take to the idea of swimming back to Cornwall.

The next few hours were the worst that I have spent at sea despite my experience as a seafaring soul. At first the boat was eerily quiet. The mainsail had been stowed and Harry used the smaller to steer the ship up and over the waves – when they came. We watched and waited. The sail flapped lazily as the sky turned purple and ugly black clouds barrelled towards the ship, bobbing like a tiny cork on the measureless ocean. The Zennor Mermaid began to roll gently as the swell increased and my stomach rolled sympathetically with the movement. The little boat began to rock and shudder as we struggled up bigger and bigger waves, only to slam down once more into the trough on the other side – over and over again. Soon the waves were the size of two-storey houses and it took all Harry's strength to hold the rudder and steer us into the waves. If one of those house-sized waves hit us from the side, it would roll us right over and the Mermaid would sink to a watery grave, taking us with her. It wasn't much to look forward to.

The wind howled and the remaining canvas sail struggled in its lines. Harry bent over to stroke my nose that poked from beneath the boy's oilskin. "Best place for you, little maid," he said gruffly and pulled my ears gently. He laid his heavy hand on the boy's head and smiled reassuringly.

That storm blew hard all night across the Atlantic and savaged our little boat in swirl of purple-black cloud mountains and rain that drummed solidly onto the wooden deck. The boy sat hunched in the prow of the boat and I curled up next to him, shivering with cold and, I admit, some fright.

The rolling of the ship got worse and worse and several times I felt sure that we would go under a wave and never come up again. But each time the Mermaid bravely struggled free of the waves and plunged on in the boiling sea. Over the sounds of the unequal battle against a furious and vengeful Mother Nature, I could just hear Harry's voice repeating the same prayer over and over again,

"Yea, though I walk through the valley of death, I shall fear no evil."

It seems that Harry's prayer was answered because we, and the Mermaid survived the storm. The sail had ripped down the middle and much of the rigging hung in tatters, but we were safe.

We limped homewards with our one good sail and were but half a day from Cornwall when Harry spied a French warship on the horizon.

"They'll be looking for us," he said. "We'll have to make a dash for it. If we're lucky, we'll run into a Navy vessel. I wouldn't even mind seeing the Customs or Excise boys today."

But when we did see a second sail, it was not the Navy. It was not the Customs Men nor the Excise Men – it was Ahmad the Terrible.

Our little boat was caught between the wrath of two mighty nations – and we were the prize.

Harry raised the sail and the little boat crashed through the lively sea. The boy sobbed quietly in the corner and I knew not how to comfort him. I licked his small, pale hand to find that it tasted salty. My heart swelled with pity for the young puppy and I climbed on to his knee to show him what affection I could. My fur was soon wet through with his tears.

An hour passed and although we had made good progress, it was not enough. As the two ships closed on us I stood at the prow of our little boat ready to defend Harry and the boy and to repel all boarders. The ships were now so close that I could see the faces of the Frenchies and also of Ahmad's men. I feared we would be crushed between the two vessels and I could tell that Harry feared the same. But there was no way we could outrun either. We had to take our chances. I closed my eyes and prayed with all my might.

Suddenly I was thrown from my paws and landed heavily on the floor of the boat as it shuddered violently beneath me. A savage 'b-boom' pounded the air and I thought I'd gone deaf. Harry put his hands over his ears and the boy did the same, trying to hide from the terrible noise. A French cannonball had smashed into the side of Ahmad's ship sending a shower of deadly splinters and shards of oak into the air.

The race was no longer about who would reach us first, but which leviathan could destroy the other.

Ahmad's crew poured onto the deck, armed with knives, swords, pistols, boarding pikes and grappling hooks. They returned cannon fire, but the pirates were not as disciplined a crew, and for every cannonball they sent crashing into their enemies, the Frenchies sent two back.

It was clear that the pirates were out-gunned by the Frenchies. The vicious pounding could not go on forever. I feared less a stray ball would land on our boat and sink us utterly, but so far the two warships had been intent on killing as many of their foes as they could. They ignored us and I supposed we were thought the booty of the victors.

The French cannon fell silent and I could see that they were preparing to board the pirate ship. At the blast of a whistle, the French sailors threw their grappling hooks into the pirates' rigging and pushed hastily-made boarding ladders across the side, covering the distance between the two ships. Musket fire from the French quarterdeck rained down on the pirates, sweeping them aside.

I watched Ahmad run shrieking and grinning as he swung his curved sword into the face of an on-coming Frenchie who'd scrambled up the thick tar-covered ropes that now dangled from the web of grappling hooks. I closed my eyes but not quickly enough and I glimpsed teeth and blood and bone flying in a spray of gristle across Ahmad's robes. He howled and cackled and ran on. Ruthless and heartless as he was, Ahmad was no coward.

He snarled at another Frenchman who tried to board the stricken pirate ship and aimed his pistol. The lead shot went wildly into the air as another cannonball hit the deck. Ahmad was the first to regain his balance and ended the Frenchman's days for good at the business end of a boarding pike.

One pirate who was nearer to us, leapt over the side, landing awkwardly in our boat. Whether he intended to use our boat to escape in or to claim our capture was not clear. That he had murderous intentions was. Harry grabbed for his pistol, but he was too slow and off balance. Smiling, the pirate pointed a pistol straight at Harry's favourite head and started to pull the trigger.

But the pirate had made one miscalculation. He had forgotten about me! He did not know that Harry's life meant more to me than my own and I would not let a scurvy pirate hurt my best friend in the whole world.

Almost without thinking, but with every instinct howling at me to save Harry, I launched myself at the pirate's arm and sank in my teeth. No longer baby teeth, but strong, white, adult teeth, I had a good grip. The man shrieked and dropped the pistol, which released the bullet on impact, sending deadly splinters shooting past my nose; but I hung on. Making the most of the pirate's predicament, Harry scooped up an oar and swung it hard at the pirate. The force of the blow sent the scurvy varmint tumbling over the boat's side. I let go just in time, landing splayed out and winded on the deck.

"Well done, little maid," gasped Harry. "I thought I was done for then but you saved me; you saved us all."

There was no need to say more and no time either. The battle was at its hottest and it was time for us to go.

On every inch of deck pirates and sailors were locked in combat, slipping and sliding in pools of dark blood. In the chaos of smoke and noise, Harry tried to manoeuvre our little boat away from the fighting giants. We were in danger of being

swamped, and, if Ahmad's boat went down, we were in severe danger of being dragged down with it.

In desperation Harry grabbed the oars, trying to row us out of danger. The boy grabbed a second pair of oars and added his childish muscles to our flight. And I? What did I do? I could do nothing to help them but urge them on with all my heart.

Behind us, I heard a cry of victory from the French – the enemy ship was sinking and pirates were jumping into the churning, frothing water. Some tried to climb the lines hanging from the French warship, but they were being cut down, or those who managed to scramble to the top were pushed back over the sides, left to a watery death and an open invitation to die in Davy Jones' locker.

We were so near to the Cornish coast now. I could see the desperation in Harry's eyes, the sweat pouring down his face as he threw every ounce of his failing strength into getting us to shore.

"Damn you!" cried a voice.

I turned and scanned the sea, trying to find the source of the voice.

Less than fifty yards behind us one of the pirates was swimming towards us, leaving a trail of crimson in his wake.

With a jolt, I realised that I recognised the figure. It was Ahmad and even in his wounded and reduced state, he still cursed us, refusing to ask for our help, though it was a stark choice between being rescued by us and death.

"Damn you!" he cried again.

Harry paused in his exertions and the feelings of pity, hatred, humanity and fear played over his honest face. He reached into the bottom of the boat and picked up a coil of rope and threw it towards Ahmad.

It seemed as if Ahmad would refuse our help, but then he grabbed the rope and Harry pulled him in towards our boat.

In the distance a ragged cheer went up from the French as the remains of the pirates' ship disappeared beneath the waves for good.

I cannot help say but that I felt relief and gratitude – that the evil pirates' trade in slaves was finished – at least for this gang of bloodthirsty, cut throat, heartless villains.

Ahmad lay silently in the belly of the boat as Harry continued to row us towards safety. We were now too near the jagged rocks of the Cornish coast to fear that the French would follow us.

Ahmad was terribly wounded – a piece of French lead had passed through his stomach. Only his indomitable will and hatred of the world had given him the strength to live this long.

As we rounded the headland that lead to Prussia Cove, the wind picked up and carried us towards the shore. Waiting there was John and Meg, the two girls, Tom and the rest of Harry's men, no doubt attracted by the sounds of a sea battle taking place just a mile off the coast.

Harry sagged with relief, his strength almost totally drained from him, even as Ahmad's blood ran darkly into the bottom of the boat.

John and his men waded into the sea and pulled the Mermaid onto the gently sloping beach of Prussia Cove.

"Brother mine!" cried John. "You're safe. I prayed to find you thus but never believed it could be so!"

The two men embraced and John helped Harry from the boat. Shem carried the boy and Jacob picked me up with one hand, remarking kindly on how much I'd grown.

Harry simply said that the boy was an orphan he had met in France. The boy hung limply in Shem's arms, exhaustion, fear and worry claiming him.

Two other men carried Ahmad gently from the boat.

"Who's this?" asked John.

Harry paused before answering. "'Tis Francis – Tommy Pellew's son," he said. Then continued as the others stared at him in amazement, "It's a long story."

"Am I... am I... home?" gasped Ahmad, struggling to sit up.

"Yes, you're in Cornwall," replied Harry, "you're home."

"Home!" gasped Ahmad, a smile drifting across his face. He lay still and breathed no more.

CHAPTER 9

From here to there…
and back again

Even though he had acted with impunity, he had, nevertheless, been one of a criminal organisation, so that his words and deeds would always have to be extremely circumspect outside the immediate family circle.

From *Smuggler, Captain Harry Carter* by Frank Pollard

In a quiet corner of a Cornish graveyard was laid to rest the mortal remains of Francis Pellew, also known as Ahmad the Terrible.

Harry held his tongue about Ahmad's rule of terror and let his grieving family believe that he had died escaping the shackles of Barbary pirates to whom he had been enslaved – which was not altogether untrue.

On our return to Prussia Cove, John pulled Harry aside and spoke earnestly to him.

"It's about the boy, Harry," he said. "Folk are beginning to ask questions and some are more interested than they should be – nosy beggars! I've even heard that Ole Ned has been sniffing around – and you know he don't think too kindly on you. Folk want to know what a French boy is doing here: where he comes from and who he be; they can tell he's not like us. Some think he's a spy, but it won't be long before they begin to approach the truth – that his father was the King of France! What's more,

Frenchies have been seen up and down the coast and some have even come ashore asking about a young boy who has been stolen away by Cornish smugglers. People are pointing the finger at you. We have to get rid of him – for all our sakes."

Harry bowed his head. He knew his brother spoke the truth, but what John didn't understand was that the three of us had been bonded together as close as family by shared experiences and 'twas hard for us to say goodbye.

But when we got back to the Carter family home at Prussia Cove, Harry changed his mind. The stout wooden door had been smashed in and the sign above hung crookedly, one chain completely torn loose. The house had been ransacked, with furniture and belongings tossed randomly about the rooms. Somebody had been looking for something – but they hadn't found it. It seemed certain they'd be back.

Meg crossed herself, glaring at the scene of the devastation, and threw a furious look at Harry as if he were to blame for her present misfortunes.

"Frenchies!" whispered Harry and John nodded in agreement.

"Thank the Lord we weren't here when they called," he said. "Francis Pellew did us a rare favour by being buried today. You must get rid of the boy. Tonight!"

And so we made our arrangements. Meg and the children were bundled off to relatives who lived inland and would, therefore, be safe from marauding Frenchies. John was to travel north up the Great Road to London as speedily as possible. With him he carried the splendid emerald and diamond ring as his passport to reach King George of England.

From thence, John would escort the King's men to meet Harry, the boy and me at a hidden location, agreed in advance. We would hide until his arrival, a wait of some ten days or so.

John rode away mounted on Jethro and I was glad that he would have such a trusty companion for his dangerous journey.

With the house strangely silent, we packed our few necessaries and waited for high tide, then Harry, the boy and I set sail once more in the Zennor Mermaid. It was surprisingly pleasant to be back on board with the mended sail that smelt strongly of bootblack (used to darken it for our present mission), rendering it invisible against the night sky.

Harry eased the little boat out of Prussia Cove and headed east, hugging the coastline instead of heading straight out to sea. The dark cliffs loomed above us and every now and then the white surf showed where rocks were hidden beneath the surface of the water. This sea was a killing ground for sailors, except for one who knew it as well as Harry. The Frenchies would not risk coming this close to shore.

I was somewhat surprised when our voyage lasted less than an hour and Harry was soon leaping out into the surf to drag the Mermaid onto a sandy beach and secure her with a piece of rope thrust through a loop of rusting iron that had been hammered in to a large granite bolder. A casual traveller would never have spotted the iron loop nor the Mermaid, which was obscured by cliffs on one side and rocks on t'other.

Suddenly, I was all a-quiver yet stood rooted to the spot, one paw raised in the air, my nostrils twitching. Could it be? Could it really be? My keen nose had led me to a fantastic discovery... a whole crate of garlic sausages washed up on the beach! My lucky star had not deserted me after all!

I ran over to the wooden box and snuffled hungrily around it. Harry and the boy approached the box with more caution; not having my unusual powers of olfaction, they remained uncertain as to what had caused my jubilant behaviour.

Harry pulled up a corner of the box and breathed deeply.

"Blimey!" said Harry, frowning.

"Sacré bleu!" said the boy, smiling.

And I wagged my tail happily. Our stay in this secret place was going to be more pleasurable than I had imagined.

Harry dragged the crate up the beach and hid it among the sand dunes.

"It'll keep well enough there," he said, one eye on me, "till we need it."

I was sad because garlic sausage was one of my favourite things in all the world – I thought it unkind to have it sitting there un-tasted.

As we climbed slowly to the top of the dunes, I suddenly realised that I knew this place. By some inadvertent hand of fate, we had returned to the place of my birth; Pengersick Castle loomed blackly against the moonlit sky. I had come home.

As I have four legs to myself, and they had only four between them, I felt I was by far the best equipped of the three to lead our party, so I scampered up the overgrown path that led to the castle's entrance and called to my mother, brother and sisters. But I was not greeted with the sound of pattering feet, only my own voice echoing back at me. The castle appeared deserted. Perhaps the ghosts had got them after all. Disappointment flooded through me but I did not have the words to explain to Harry. I stood with my tail sagging and sorrow etched on my face.

Then, to my surprise, I heard a faint scuffling of feet below the ground. I cocked my head to one side and listened carefully. Harry looked at me enquiringly.

I let out a playful bark. There was a pause, then a rush of feet and a pair of dark brown eyes, so like my own, peeped out from the castle's ruined doorway.

Barking happily, I ran towards the castle entrance and embraced my dear mother, receiving a thorough licking in return.

Behind her, popping out like corks from the secret passageway came one, two, three, four furry heads – my brothers and sisters, companions and play fellows of my youth.

Harry called out in alarm, thinking, at first, that I was being attacked. Then he remarked on the similarities between us and stood scratching his head.

"So this is your family, is it, little one? And a fine crew they are, too. I hope they will give me as warm a welcome!"

Once I explained to my family about Harry and the boy, my mother allowed them into the castle and I showed Harry the secret passageway; a fine place to hide, should it be needed.

My family crowded around me and sat spellbound whilst I recounted my adventures with Harry up until the present day. Then, in turn, I listened to their history since my departure some nine months beforehand.

Two of my brothers, George and Jack, had gone to live on a farm and were having a fine time of it, with fresh milk every day and meat three times a week.

Sister Jenna had been taken in by a spinster, widow of a fisherman, and helped to catch rabbits for the cooking pot.

Bryok and Cadan had gone to live with the vicar of Breage and were getting fat on donations from the parishioners.

When it came to tell of Morvoren, mother bowed her head in sadness. My youngest and fairest sister had gone out one fine, sunny day and never returned. Not a whisper had been heard of her for some three months.

I hoped, that like me, she had gone to make her fortune and

would one day return, bearing gifts.

Gifts! As soon as the thought struck me, I realised that I could indeed supply gifts to my dear family.

Wagging my smuggler's tail, I ran down to the beach with my brothers and sisters hot on my heels and mother bringing up

the rear. I dug through the dunes until I uncovered the crate of garlic sausages and presented it to them.

The expression on their faces as they tasted their first garlic sausage was delightful indeed.

It was very pleasant lying on the cool sand eating garlic

sausages with my family, but my conscience pricked me, so I scooped up the final string of sausages and took them back to the boy, trying hard not to catch Harry's eye on my return.

The days that followed were some of the happiest of my young life. The boy and I spent the days exploring the old castle and I showed him many of my favourite hiding places, including the secret passageway. It was now partially collapsed but had, at one time, led down to a cave on the beach. I was still small enough to squeeze through the gap left by the fallen masonry, but only someone with four legs could move down the tunnel in comfort.

Harry spent the mornings fishing for our lunch and the evenings watching the horizon with his brass telescope from the castle's square tower. Harry also considered how best to defend the castle, should the Frenchies find us before the King's men. Hiding was the favoured option, and Harry made sure that the boy knew that the secret passageway would be his place. Not unnaturally, given his recent incarceration, the boy had a fear of dark, lonely places and was reluctant to leave Harry's side. But Harry assured him that he would not be alone as my remaining brothers and sisters had adopted the boy as one of their own and, indeed, at times I myself thought of him as a younger brother, a puppy.

The peace of our happy band was shattered early one morning, some eight days after our first arrival. From the castellated tower Harry spotted a foreign sail on the horizon.

"Frenchies!" he said, his face set in a grim line.

"Per'aps they will not come 'ere," said the boy.

"Perhaps," replied Harry, but he didn't sound hopeful and continued to watch the progress of the strangers.

Slowly but surely the vessel closed upon our lonely beach.

"They're coming straight for us," said Harry, looking worried. "Somebody has blabbed."

When the crew started loading themselves into small rowing boats it was certain that they were coming for us. We went about making the castle as secure as possible. Our refuge would be in the tower itself: the walls were of thick granite and would easily withstand musket fire. Moreover, the ship's cannon could not easily reach us, for the castle was in a slight dip and not even the top of the tower could be seen from the sea; it was clear that the sailors would never get enough elevation to loose their cannon upon us. Having lived through one sea battle I knew that a ship's cannon was useful for one thing – pounding the living daylights from another vessel; but they were not made for land bombardments.

I estimated that our attackers numbered fifty and I could see from the grim look on Harry's face that he had also come to a similar conclusion. Our defence lay in the thick castle walls and the hopes and prayers of one man, a boy and six fur-bearing companions – easily a match for the Frenchies.

Harry stoked the flames in the Solar room's great fireplace; he was boiling seawater. We did not have a barrel of tar or hot oil to throw down the stone chute, called most aptly 'a murder hole', but boiling seawater would slow attackers in their tracks and no mistake.

The boy had a pile of large rocks and other building rubble that he had collected over the past week; his plan was to throw the missiles at the attackers – Harry wanted him to stay hidden but the boy was prepared to fight for his freedom and so was I. Should the attackers break through our defences, neither the boy nor Harry would find me wanting.

The plan was that my mother, brother Goron, brother

Henna, sister Susan, sister Rosenwyn and myself would harass and slow the attackers some distance from the castle. Biting ankles, calves and hands, we would use our superior speed and diminutive size to get back to the castle through the secret passageway and continue the assault should any make it past the castle's solid oak door. It would buy Harry and the boy time – but not much.

As the first boatload of attackers made land, our small pack came tearing over the dunes barking furiously and baring our teeth and snapping at any exposed flesh. Brother Henna fastened his teeth around a plump calf and the Frenchie howled in pain. Mother launched herself at a small knot of sailors who retreated so quickly that two of the varmints fell backwards into the water lapping at their ankles. Susan and Rosenwyn joined me in leaping on their prostrate bodies and biting them hard. Cursing with pain and fury, the remainder of the Frenchies ran for their vessel and brother Goron outdid us all by leaping into their boat, causing several Frenchies to jump overboard, thus causing the maximum confusion and panic. Then he boldly dived from the boat and swam back to us and we lay helpless with laughter on the beach.

The first attack had been successfully repulsed.

The second attack was pressed much harder as the Frenchies were now alerted to our presence. Six men stood with loaded muskets whilst the others attempted to disembark. But we were small targets and could run and dodge as fast as summer lightning. We slowed their progress but as the second and then the third boatload began to disembark, we were overcome by the sheer weight of numbers.

"Kill the whelp!" yelled a voice in terror. I looked up, recognising Ole Ned's unwashed form. I tried to get to him to show him what I thought of traitors but was driven back by more and more sailors leaping from the boats.

Rosenwyn received a vicious kick to the ribs and ran off yelping. Mother, too, had been wounded and was limping badly. I rounded on her attacker, paying him in kind for his mistreatment of my mother. I left him short a finger or two, whimpering in pain and unable to fire his musket. I smiled grimly – the battle would not be all one way, despite our being heavily outnumbered.

Dogging their footsteps and driving them into a white frenzy, the Frenchies made slow progress towards the castle, but time and numbers were on their side. Eventually, worn down, injured and exhausted, I acknowledged that it was time to leave, and barked the signal for retreat. We slipped unseen into the secret passageway and lay there some minutes licking our wounds and recovering our breath.

I went to report to Harry, but he had seen for himself our noble battle and hot, salty tears leaked from his eyes when he saw our pitiable state. Gently he wrapped Susan's broken ribs in a soft, white cloth and bathed mother's bleeding paw in warm seawater, then bandaged it carefully. I licked his hand with gratitude and he buried his face in my warm fur and thanked me from the bottom of his heart.

But the fight was not over yet.

A voice called from without the castle.

"Harry Carter! We don't want you. Just send out the boy and you will not be harmed."

"I won't be harmed if I stay in here, either," replied Harry fiercely, "and I'll not send out the boy."

"Then you will die," said the icy voice.

"Brave words! Brave words indeed," cried Harry, "from a man

who has odds of fifty-to-one on his side. You're a big man, aren't you?! Why don't you try and take the boy from me? Cowards! The lot of you! All these men needed for one small boy!"

"The boy is the son of a king who betrayed his people and led them into poverty and starvation," replied the voice. "He must join his father on the guillotine."

"He's just a boy!" cried Harry, "A child-vean! Is there no pity in your heart?"

"Send out the boy and save yourself," continued the remorseless voice, "or you will die."

There was nothing more to be said. Harry would no sooner have sent out the boy to meet his death than I. It was war.

A group of hard faced Frenchies pounded at the old, oak door, which creaked uneasily on its ancient hinges. Harry poured the boiling seawater down on them, scalding several, causing them to shriek and curse. The boy stood on the castle's tower and hurled down stones, breaking the heads of several, until they learned to cover their heads with pieces of sailcloth, which slowed them mightily.

When Harry's supply of boiling seawater ran out and the boy's collection of stones had thinned, we knew there was little time left. Mother led the way as Harry forced the boy into the secret passageway and covered the opening hastily. Then with Henna, Rosenwyn, Goron, Susan and I at his side, Harry mounted the granite steps and waited at the top of the castle's tower, his cutlass grasped in one hand and his pistol in the other.

The stone stairs were configured to the advantage of the defender; anyone trying to get up the stairs would not be able to easily wield a sword, whereas Harry was able to swing his cutlass freely with his right hand. Those long dead Cornish fighting men had known what they were about and Pengersick

Castle defended itself even in its present dilapidated state – I was sure that even the ghosts were on our side, although they were sadly lacking in visibly aiding us. Perhaps they were lonely and secretly hoped for new companions. I shrugged off the thought even as a shudder ran through me.

The ancient oak door could not take much more pounding and the Frenchies were even firing their lead muskets into the tough old wood. But it would not be too long before they battered their way through the groaning door.

Suddenly, the Frenchies yelled out and I knew we had but minutes to live. We stood, tense and alert, but the attackers did not come. Instead their voices were directed away from the castle. I peered out of an arrow slit and gaped at the sight in front of me. Two platoons of heavily armed English cavalry were bearing down on the French. Riding at their head was John Carter himself in a florid red coat, screaming oaths in Cornish. I hardly dared believe it, but we were saved!

Harry leapt down the steps two at a time and wrenched open the damaged door. The cavalry were chasing the Frenchies across the dunes and back to their boats. They were sent packing, along with Ole Ned, howling and shrieking.

John was staring anxiously at the tower when Harry appeared in the doorway with me at his side.

"You're safe!" cried John.

"You're late!" replied Harry as the two brothers embraced and dear Jethro nuzzled Harry's shoulder.

In the distance the sound of shots still rang out, but the battle was clearly over. The officer in charge trotted back breathing heavily.

"Good morning, Mr Carter," said the man, doffing his plumed helmet with a flourish. "I am Captain Richard Lewis of

His Majesty's Household Cavalry," said the man. "I apologise for our tardy arrival."

"'Twas close," admitted Harry, "but you are very welcome, sir."

"And where is his Royal Highness the Dauphin of France?"

Harry frowned and then realised that Captain Lewis was talking about the boy. "Young Louis? He's right here!" and Harry uncovered the secret passageway to reveal two pairs of anxious eyes: the boy sat with his arms around my mother, who was licking his face calmly. The boy crawled out blinking into the daylight.

"We 'ave won, 'Arry?" asked the boy.

"That we have, son," said Harry and the boy threw his arms around Harry's neck and hugged him tightly.

There was quite a commotion when the boy refused to go to London with Captain Lewis unless Harry went, too.

"You has to go," said Harry softly. "Your people need you and the King of England can help you. You has to leave here and go to London."

"Come with me, 'Arry," begged the child prince.

"I can't!" said Harry, "I belong here and you belong with them. I wouldn't be happy in London and you can't stay here."

"Yes! Yes I can!" cried the boy, "I can stay 'ere and live with you."

Harry sighed deeply and I knew he was tempted to agree with the boy for he had come to love him as a son.

"Boy," said Harry, "it burns my heart to say it, but you must go with Captain Lewis. I cannot protect you here and…" (He waved away the boy's protest), "and you would endanger my family if you stayed – and that I cannot allow."

The boy hung his head and his lip trembled.

My mother, who was waiting nearby, limped up to the boy and licked his hand.

"Will you come with me?" said the boy, and my dear, sweet mother wagged her tail.

And so it was that mother, Susan, Goron, Henna and Rosenwyn went to live in a palace with a prince. I was sorry indeed to see them go but glad to know they would be fat and happy and well cared for until the end of their days. I was also glad to know that the boy would have the most faithful, loyal and trustworthy bodyguard in the whole world – my family.

Sadly, we waved the party goodbye. The boy turned in his saddle and watched us for a long time.

It seemed an empty sort of victory as John and Harry packed up our things ready for the short journey back to Prussia Cove. John would travel with Jethro by road and Harry and I were to sail back on the Mermaid.

I wondered if a present would cheer up Harry. I find that presents always make me feel a good deal more cheerful and so I recovered the string of garlic sausages that I had saved for a rainy day. A broad smile on Harry's tired face was my reward and Harry hugged me close.

"Thank you, little shipmate," he said. "Time to be going now."

We turned our backs on the castle and the scene of our famous victory and sailed for home.

The ghosts of Pengersick Castle were left to dream in peace.

Endnote

Harry made himself a home just a few miles from Prussia Cove at a place called Rinsey where he stayed for the rest of his life. When he wrote his autobiography in 1809, the Carter brothers were still working and Harry, though ostensibly a tenant farmer and preacher, was still a partner, busy with the office end of the family business. Neither he, nor his brother nor any of the others of their smuggler band died rich; but there is no doubt that he was happy in his own way.

Ole Ned, I heard, was suitably punished and spent the remainder of his days in Devon.

I never heard what became of the Dauphin and he never regained the crown of France that was rightly his, but I wish to believe he lived a quiet and happy life in England, with my dear family, for the rest of his days.

As for me, I found I had gained a thirst for adventure and was ready to meet the road ahead with a straight eye and a spring in my step. After all, it was just the beginning...

La Bandida
– Pip goes to Mexico

Pip's adventures take her to the land of Aztec treasure at the end of the eighteenth century.

How can Pip unlock the magic of the mysterious and deadly crystal skull? How can a Cornish maid survive in the hostile and mountainous land? Fighting off cougars, coyotes and bandits, Pip makes her way across Mexico searching for the lost treasure of an ancient civilization.

(Not yet published)

Tartu and the Pharaoh's Curse

Working on an archaeological dig in Egypt with her Uncle Howard, Tartu stumbles across the secret burial chamber of an ancient Pharaoh, uncovering a glittering treasure horde – and a deadly secret.

On her journey from the pyramids of Cairo to the catacombs of Alexandria, Tartu meets a kaleidoscope of memorable characters including the shambling camel Ata Allah; Dolly the donkey; Rhakotisa, the mad parrot of Alexandria; Alfred the army chimp (who is a bit too fond of home made dynamite); and Tartu's dear friend and staunch companion, the elderly daredevil bulldog, Colonel Corpus Crunch.

Tartu races against time to solve the riddle of the sands and save the people she loves from an ancient evil and terrible foe.

Tartu's Close Encounter

What really happened at Windsor Castle the night the Queen's favourite corgi was abducted? Who are the mysterious visitors and what do they want?

Tartu's investigation of these strange events uncovers a plot of otherworldly dimensions. Accompanied by a motley crew of overfed, overweight and pampered corgis, Pericles the bad-tempered parrot and Toby, gamekeeper's dog to the Royal Family, Tartu's quest takes her on a difficult and dangerous journey across the English countryside to a place of ancient power.

Her search unwittingly reveals a secret that has been hidden for thousands of years – and an old enemy returns to haunt her.

Although a complete story in its own right, *Tartu's Close Encounter* follows on from the events described in *Tartu and the Pharaoh's Curse*.

Tartu's Arctic Adventure

Battling to save the Arctic wilderness from an unscrupulous oil baron and environmental terrorist, Tartu joins forces with Naku, a husky puppy, Solomon the polar bear and Herbert, a penguin from the Antarctic who is a long way from home.

Tartu's worst nightmare is realised when her nemesis, the wolf Malvoise, vows to stop Tartu – once and for all.

(Not yet published)

Zulu Magregor
and the vultures of San Felipe

Zulu Magregor is part Japanese, part English, part Portuguese and raised in the Scottish Highlands by his grandparents.

Having just completed a doctorate in environmental science he's taking on the world's worst corporate polluters from Papua New Guinea, to Mexico, to Antarctica and beyond.

Zulu is on a mission – and it's just not healthy to get in his way.

(Not yet published)